Tame A Wild Bride

CYNTHIA WOOLF

DEDICATION

For my wonderful husband Jim. I couldn't do any of this without you. I love you, Sweetie.

ACKNOWLEDGEMENTS

For my critique partners who help me in so many more ways than just critiquing my work. You help make me a better writer and a better person. Thank you Kally Jo Surbeck, Michele Callahan, Karen Docter, Jennifer Zane and to the late CJ Snyder, rest in peace my friend.

CHAPTER 1

Rosemary Stanton stood patiently on the train platform, sweat rolling down her back and between her ample breasts. Waiting. Sweating because it was an unusually hot day in late April. Waiting for her husband. A husband she wouldn't recognize if he were standing right next to her.

She'd been desperate when she answered the advertisement for a mail order bride. *Wanted: Single woman to cook, clean, and care for children on a cattle ranch in southwestern Colorado. Will marry upon arrival.*

Well, she was twenty-six with no

prospects. Her brother just got married and his new wife, Beatrice, didn't want Rosie around. She could answer the advertisement or become a governess; help someone else's children grow up into adults; live in someone else's house, for the rest of her life, have nothing she could call her own.

Rosie wanted a home. Her own home. She wanted a husband and children. All the things she'd never have if she stayed in Philadelphia. When she'd seen the ad in the morning paper, she'd nearly shouted with glee. However, she managed to restrain herself until she retired to her room before she giggled with delight as she pressed her back against the door. The advertisement was tailor-made for her needs. It got her away from Beatrice and got her her own home all in one fell swoop.

Her brother, Robert, was not happy with the idea of his baby sister traveling across the country to marry a stranger. He grudgingly agreed to give her her dowry to take with her—five thousand dollars. She'd take the draft to the bank as soon as she arrived in Creede, Colorado, and married Mr. Thomas Harris, cattle rancher. It was her "in case it doesn't work out" money. Though she supposed it would belong to her husband once she married. Perhaps she just wouldn't tell him about it.

Her conscience spoke up. *That's no way to start a marriage. With lies and secrets.* Oh, all right. She'd tell him and have him take her to the bank. But not until after she'd taken his measure. She could tell by how he treated his animals what kind of man he was. A man who was cruel to his horses would also be cruel to his wife. If he was a cruel man, she would leave and she sure as heck wouldn't tell him about her money.

Even the substantial size of her dowry couldn't seem to provide marriage prospects for Rosie back in Philadelphia. She wasn't pretty in the conventional sense. She thought her face with its big brown eyes and full lips was pleasing enough, but men apparently hadn't. Her one beau told her that her eyes were the color of warm brandy. That was before he left her to marry another more *suitable* woman. More suitable, hah! Richer was more like it.

He'd had expensive tastes and had married a rabbit-faced girl, heir to a substantial fortune to which he'd have access. Well, good luck and good riddance.

She hoped her new husband wouldn't be as snootish as Paul had been. As a cattle rancher, she didn't know what to expect but the idea of a more earthy, less frivolous man appealed to her.

Rosie did have one extraordinary feature. Her hair. Waist length, wavy and a clear, golden blonde. Right now, standing on the train platform in Creede, it was bound up in a loose bun on top of her head under her hat. It, like the rest of her, was covered in white dirt and a nasty grayish soot from the train. Her suit would never be the same again.

She'd discovered on the second day of her trip, she could minimize the grime by sitting in the front of the car with the window closed. But sooner or later the heat and mugginess of the car would force her to open the window. The air came rushing in, cooling her, but bringing with it the dirt and ash from the train's boilers and whatever the wind picked up along the way.

On the long trip, she'd told herself again and again she'd made the right decision. She was right to make the difficult trip. This was her life and she had to take her future into her own hands.

"Excuse me. Miss Stanton?"

Rosie shaded her eyes from the late afternoon sun and looked up at a tall man with dark hair. His hat was pulled low, hiding his eyes. He had a strong jaw covered with a shadow of whiskers.

"Yes. I'm Rosemary Stanton."

He took off his hat and held out his hand. "I'm Tom Harris."

Rosie took his hand. It engulfed hers with a shock of warmth. Her pale skin stood in stark contrast to his tanned one. Calluses rubbed against her soft palm, though the touch was not unpleasant. She looked from their clasped hands up into the bluest eyes she'd ever seen.

"Pleased to meet you, Mr. Harris."

"Tom. Call me Tom."

"And I'm Rosie."

"Where are your trunks, Rosie?"

"Oh, I don't have any trunks. I only brought what I thought I would need out here."

He picked up the two valises at her feet. "Doesn't seem like much for an Eastern woman. I'm glad to see you're practical."

Rosie felt the heat in her cheeks and knew she blushed at his praise, undeserving as it was. "Well, I didn't think you'd have any balls."

He cocked an eyebrow.

"No, I didn't mean…I meant…well, no need for fancy gowns or dresses." Mortified clear down to her toes, she hoped the platform would just open up and swallow her now. "I'm sorry, I'm rambling. I do that when I'm nervous."

"Do I make you nervous, Rosie?" His deep baritone swept over her, caressing her, soothing her.

"Yes. No." She shook her head, hoping to jiggle something sensible loose. "It's the situation which makes me nervous."

He nodded knowingly. "The wedding ceremony. Well, that is one thing you don't have to worry about anymore. We're going to the preacher's house now to get it done."

Rosie was surprised. Shocked was more like it. "Now? I mean, I thought we might talk a while. Take a couple of days…"

"No time for that. I have to get back to the ranch. We'll stay tonight at Peabody's Boarding House. The owner, Mary Peabody, is a friend of mine. The rooms are always clean and she serves the best food in town. I always stay there, if she has an opening, when I come to town. Tomorrow, we'll go pick up my kids from the McKenzie's and head to the ranch. By the time we get home, you'll barely have time to cook supper before it's dark and time to put Ben and Suzie to bed."

Rosie had hoped they'd have some time to get to know each other before they got married. Heck, she'd have been happy with a bath before her wedding. She understood she couldn't go live at his ranch without being married to him. It would be unseemly. Her reputation would be in shambles, and who would want to marry a woman with a bad reputation? Especially if you had children. It would rub off on you, but more importantly, on them. So an immediate marriage was necessary. She understood all of that, but it didn't change what she wished for.

"You can cook, can't you? In your letters you said you were a good cook."

She nodded her head. "I *am* a good cook. I've never had a complaint."

"Good. Glad to hear it. Shall we go?"

She took a deep breath; scared out of her wits she was making a mistake. "Yes. I suppose we should."

They walked to the waiting buckboard. He put her bags in the back and helped her up on to it for the trip to the preachers. She was much relieved to see that his horses were well cared for.

*****

The marriage ceremony was short, thank God. Rosie stood next to Tom, grime covering her from head to toe. No place to even wash her face. Sweat formed in rivulets down her temples. She'd tried to keep her face and hands clean while traveling, but they came upon Creede, the end of the line, without her being able to check her appearance and wash up again. Not that it would have made much difference. Her traveling gloves, normally black, were ash colored from the dirt and grime of the last five days. Thanks to her gloves and the fact she wore them most of the time, her hands were relatively clean.

Tendrils of hair hung down all over, having escaped from their restraints. She'd so carefully put up all of her hair into a bun high atop her head at the start of the trip. Now she was sure she looked like some sort of rag-a-muffin, and this was her wedding day. Her dreams about her wedding didn't include her being dirty and wearing a traveling suit that was four days past feeling fresh. She'd brought her dress, thinking she'd have a real wedding. But that's all it was, a dream. Mentally slapping herself, she remembered this *wasn't* a dream, this was reality. A reality she'd chosen, so she lifted her chin a little higher and made the best of it.

When they got to the rings, Tom placed a plain gold band on her finger. She had her father's wedding band to give to him. It was also gold, but had scroll work etched into it.

Then the preacher said "You may kiss the bride." Tom looked at her and, as if he were seeing her for the first time, searched her face, probably trying to find a clean place to kiss her. He finally leaned down and gave her a chaste kiss on the lips. Quick, but not so fast she didn't feel the warmth of his lips on hers all the way to her toes. She could get used to that.

They arrived at the boardinghouse, as newlyweds, just in time for supper. Mary Peabody, a short, white-haired lady, had the table laden with food. It sat twelve and, with Tom and Rosie, was packed. It was Thursday night and apparently Thursday was fried steak night. Mashed potatoes and gravy, fresh biscuits, green beans flavored with pieces of bacon, creamed onions and baked apples shared the table.

"Mary, this is Rosie, my wife," Tom said by way of introduction.

Rosie's mouth watered at the delicious aromas assaulting her from the table.

Mary seemed oblivious to Rosie's grimy condition as she took Rosie's hand in both of hers. "Pleased to meet you, Rosie."

"As I am you," said Rosie. "Do you have some place I could wash up? I'm afraid I'm still covered with grime from the train."

"Why sure, hon, follow me."

Mary led the way to the kitchen. "There's a basin at the sink, hot water in the kettle, and I'll get you a towel."

"Thank you," said Rosie, ecstatic she'd be able to wash her face with soap and water. "There's only so much you can do with a handkerchief."

"Don't I know it." Mary handed her a

dish towel. "I've traveled to Denver a couple of times and felt like I'd been rolling in a pile of dirt by the time I got there. I can't imagine being on a train for days on end. Tom told me before that you were coming from Philadelphia. That's a big change...coming to Creede. Sure you're up to it?"

Rosie washed and dried her face. "I know I am. I want a home and children. I'm determined to make this work."

"Glad to hear it. Tom doesn't need anymore tragedy in his life."

Rosie nodded. "I understand he's a widower."

"He's more than that."

"What do you mean?

Mary looked a little flustered. "I've already said too much. I'll let him tell you."

"Of course, I should get that kind of information from my husband. That sounds so strange to say. Um, do you think I could get a bath after supper?"

"I'll arrange to have it readied for you. You just tell me when you want it sent up."

"Splendid. Anytime after supper would be wonderful. Thank you."

"It's nothing. Now, let's go eat supper before it's cold or all eaten."

Rosie laughed.

Tom stood when they entered and held her chair out for her.

Rosie had never been a picky eater. She wasn't willow thin. She was full bodied and strong. She used to help the maids clean the house, much to her brother's chagrin, but it kept her from turning to fat, as so many of her friends were doing.

She glanced over at Tom. His hair so deep, dark brown, as to be almost black. His blue eyes blazed against his tanned skin. He had crow's feet, probably from the sun. He didn't appear to be the type that laughed too often. Perhaps she could change that.

Tom was tall and lean, not skinny, but

muscular. Even so, she was amazed at the amount of food he ate. If her brother had eaten like that, he'd have weighed three hundred pounds in no time. Still, he must work very hard if he could put away that much food and remain lean. She made a mental note to cook twice as much as she was used to cooking.

"Tell me, Tom," she said, trying to get used to saying his name instead of calling him Mr. Harris. "You said in your letters your children are aged ten and three, correct?"

"Yes. Ben is ten and Suzie is three. Why?"

Rosie leaned in toward him so she wouldn't have to shout. No need for everyone to know their business. "I was trying to determine how much food I'll need to prepare."

"You'll be cooking for fifteen. Not just the family, but the cow hands, too. Is that going to be a problem?" He took a bite of the baked apple. From the look on his face, it was very good.

"No, not at all. Fifteen. I'll have to adjust my recipes. Increase the proportions. I only cooked for my brother and a small staff of servants at home. Robert didn't want to hire a cook, so that was one of the things I did." Amend mental note: *quadruple* all recipes.

"Glad to hear it."

"Tell me about your ranch," she said as she cut her steak.

He set his fork down and almost smiled when he started talking about his ranch. "It's only a thousand acres, small compared to some of the ranches around here. I run three hundred head of cattle on it with the help of eleven men. I hire extra men during branding season and when we drive the herd to the railhead here in Creede once a year. Have you ever cooked out of a chuck wagon?"

"No." She sat up straighter, feeling a growing sense of panic. "Surely you don't expect me to go on a cattle drive with you?" she said, appalled he would even consider it.

He had the good sense to look

chastised. "No, no of course not. Old Orvie will continue to do the cooking for us on the drives."

"Obviously, I'll stay at home with the children," she added firmly.

"Just Suzie. Ben will be going on the cattle drive with me this year. It's his first time and he's looking forward to it."

"Isn't he a little young?" she asked surprised.

"Not out here. It's time he learned." He shoveled in a forkful of potatoes.

"Speaking of learning, I assume I'll be teaching the children since you are so far from town and the school. That's not something we discussed. Do you teach them now?" She took another bite of her steak. It was the most delicious she'd ever tasted. So tender it nearly melted in her mouth. She made another mental note to ask Mary what she did to make it so tender.

"My wife did up until two years ago." His bitterness was unmistakable.

Rosie assumed that was when she'd died. He'd never said in his letters when she died. He must have loved her very much to still be so bitter after all this time.

"I've been doing the best I can." he said. "I hoped you'd be willing to take it over, even though it wasn't in our agreement."

Rosie put down her fork, finished with her supper. "You and the children are my family now. Their best interests are mine as well. We want them to grow up and be able to succeed in any endeavor they choose, and they need schooling to be able to do that."

"I agree." He looked surprised that she'd be thinking of the children, but he shouldn't have. She'd made it clear in her letters she wanted children.

It was still light outside when they finished dinner. Tom suggested they go for a walk and he'd show her the town. Though she dearly wanted her bath, she thought it might be best to spend the time with her new husband. She asked Mary to wait on the bath.

17

Creede was not large by any stretch of the imagination, but there was everything necessary for a farmer, rancher, or miner. Two hotels besides the boardinghouse, a mercantile and feed store, barber shop, bank, sheriff's office, courthouse, two churches, ten saloons and several whorehouses, which she didn't stop to count. She supposed the miners, from the surrounding silver mines, had to go somewhere to spend their money and let off steam. She doubted many of them did it in church.

It took them about an hour to walk down one side of town and up the other. They walked side-by-side, but Tom made sure to keep his distance and didn't hold her hand. She really couldn't blame him considering the state of her clothes. Twilight had settled on the town by the time they got back to the boarding house.

Rosie was nervous. There was no other way to put it. Tonight was her wedding night, and she had no experience, no real idea of what would happen and what was expected of her. She wished they could wait for a while before they became intimate. She didn't think Tom would like the idea, so she was surprised by his words as they walked up the stairs to their room.

"Rosie, I know you're nervous about tonight, but you don't need to be. I'm not taking you to bed tonight. Maybe not anytime soon. But I will bed you, hell, that's what a wife is for, but just so you know, there'll be no more children. I'll see to that."

Even though she'd wanted to wait, she didn't mean forever. She was flabbergasted and hurt. He was killing her dreams. The one thing she wanted more than anything was children. Her own children.

"May I ask why?" Her voice broke as she choked out the question.

Tom was straight forward with his answer. No beating around the bush for him. "My wife left me for some sweet talkin', low-life peddler. Then she had the good taste to go and get herself killed in a carriage accident. I've got no use for a woman in my life. My children do. You're here for them. I love my children, but I don't want to be left to raise more when you leave."

Now she knew where the bitterness

came from. Not from his love for his first wife, but the woman's betrayal of him. "Not all women are as shallow and self-centered as your wife was."

"You couldn't prove it by me." His eyes blazed with anger. "If you want an annulment, now is the time to say so."

He might as well have slapped her. The pain would have been easier to take. "I don't plan on needing an annulment. I made a bargain and I'll keep it. I appreciate your *consideration* in telling me, you might have done so in our letters. Don't expect me to be happy about it. You lured me here under false pretenses, without disclosing some pertinent facts. You married me without giving me a chance to say no. Your children are mine now, but I still want a child of my own. I'm not asking for your love. And I'll never ask you for another thing."

She must have gotten to him. He answered her, "You'll never have my love or interest, but I'll consider what you've said. As for now, the fact we haven't had intercourse doesn't mean we won't appear to be a happily married couple. You will share my bed, for sleeping only, and my bedroom is now ours."

"Of course, that would be best."

When they got to their room, he opened the door and held it for her to enter, then closed it behind them. It wasn't a large room. There was a small dresser, wardrobe, commode with pitcher and basin on it, a small table with two chairs, and dominating the room, the bed.

She stared at the bed.

"It seems awful small for two people."

"You'll get used to it. You can sleep under the sheet and I'll sleep on top of it. Trust me. You're quite safe from me. Tonight."

Rosie was disappointed. He rejected her. Didn't find her attractive enough to want to have sex with her. Maybe he used a whore at one of the whorehouses. That wouldn't be something he'd tell her. Oh well, he may not want more children, but she did. She'd just have to seduce him. After all, as far as she knew there was still only one way to get pregnant. Yup, with all her feminine wiles, she could easily seduce him. Right.

"I'm sure I am." She blushed. "Mary promised me a bath, and I'd like some privacy once it gets here." She could be as detached as he was. For a while anyway, but not for long. He'd change his mind about this, or her name wasn't Rosemary Louise Stanton Harris.

CHAPTER 2

Tom knew his words hurt her. But she needed to know where he stood. She needed to know she'd never have him, never have his heart. It was for the best she didn't know how attractive he found her. Round in all the right places, which he ached to touch. And her lips. Those amazingly kissable lips she nibbled when she was nervous. He doubted she even realized she did it. And he wasn't dead after all. He may not have been with a woman in years, Sarah quit having sex with him even before she left. Said she needed her strength for the children. But that didn't mean he didn't get urges just like the next man. Maybe he should have forced her; other men would have. They would've thought it their right. But Tom wanted a woman to want him. Want to lie with him. He wouldn't force himself on a woman ever.

Still, sleeping next to her and not touching her was going to be the hardest thing he'd ever done. He'd consigned himself to hell for as long as she decided to stay. But he knew she'd leave. Women always left. Didn't Sarah prove that?

He'd stayed at the boardinghouse many times over the years. But in all those years, he'd never noticed that the beds were so darn small. He'd be touching Rosie all night if he didn't hang off the side. It was going to be torture.

"When the bath comes, I'll go for a walk to give you some privacy."

He watched her turn a pretty shade of pink from the tops of her ears all the way down her neck as far as he could see. Which wasn't far, since she had her blouse buttoned clear to the top.

"Thank you," she whispered.

There was a knock on the door.

A man carried the long metal tub into the room, setting it down in the center. He was followed by two more men with buckets of steaming water and a third with cold water. They filled the tub.

"Here you go, ma'am. Mary sent up some of her bath salts for you." He handed her a small packet.

"Thank you, and tell Mary I appreciate it."

He nodded and left.

Tom got up to leave. "Enjoy your bath. I'll be gone about a half hour, so be done by then."

She took her hair down from what was left of the bun atop her head. Once all the pins where out of it, she ran her fingers through it and shook her head to get it all loose. Tom had never seen anyone with such beautiful hair. The urge to touch it, to run his hands through it was nearly irresistible, but he managed. He turned on his heel and left before he did something he'd regret.

It felt so good to have her hair down.

She hurried out of her clothes and stepped into the tub. The water was hot and so wonderful. Her aching muscles felt better already. Rosie dunked her head and soaped up her hair. It was going to be clean for the first time in a week. Dunking her head again, she rinsed her hair and soaped up and rinsed her body.

By the time he got back, she was combing the tangles from her hair. After she got them all out, she braided it for sleeping. Plus it would add to the waves in the morning. She was going to use all her wiles to change his mind about bedding her. Maybe not tonight, she really did want to get to know him better. But he would bed her. She would have a real marriage, and hopefully the additional children she wanted.

Rosie was sitting on the bed when he came in and started to unbutton his shirt. She let out a small gasp; couldn't help it. She'd never seen a man without his clothes, all of his clothes. Knowing he was her husband and she needed to get used to his being naked sometimes, didn't stop her from being surprised. Or thrilled by what she saw.

He was muscular without having overly bulging muscles. His shoulders were wide and his chest looked hard. It was sprinkled with curly brown hair. Was it soft? Her hands ached to find out.

Rosie looked away. She'd had to. Her body yearned for something. She wasn't exactly sure for what, except she wanted to touch him. Badly. Looking away was the only thing she could do to break the spell he wove.

He looked over at her and she felt herself blush from the tops of her ears all the way down her neck. Turning his back on her, he unbuttoned his shirt and took it off. It didn't help. Seeing him from the back only emphasized the width of his shoulders and narrow waist.

"Don't worry," he said as he walked to the bed. "I'm leaving my pants on for tonight, but you're going to have to get accustomed to seeing me without clothes. Just because I'm not going to fuck you, doesn't mean I'm going to sleep in my clothes every night."

He smiled at her small nod. Sitting on

the bed, he took his boots off, doused the lamp and then laid back.

Rosie gave an inward sigh. She'd dream about his magnificent body tonight. All muscles, long and sleek. He was like a thoroughbred race horse rather than a Clydesdale. He was lean, well built and she felt his heat immediately. It was like sleeping next to a furnace. It was going to be a long night. A very long night.

*****

Warm. The bed was so warm. And hard. Her hand rested on a warm, hard…chest. Oh, God! She opened one eye and looked up into Tom's dark blue ones.

"Good morning." His voice reverberated in his chest, through her hand and straight to her core. Heating her up in places she'd never been hot before.

She backed away like something burned her, which he practically had.

He chuckled.

"I…I got cold."

"I could tell." His eyes danced with amusement.

"I'll try not to let it happen again."

"I don't mind. These things are bound to happen when you sleep with someone."

At least he wasn't totally immune to her. He didn't mind that she cuddled with him. It was a start.

"Oh." Her mouth suddenly dry, she reached for the glass of water he'd brought her last night and took a large swallow. She coughed hard as it went down her wind pipe. Tom sat up and slapped her on the back.

"Are you all right?"

She nodded and gasped for air.

"Before you choke again, I'll get my clothes on and you can dress when I'm gone." He sat on the side of the bed, and pulled on his boots, then grabbed his shirt and put it on, buttoning it as he walked out the door. "I'll get us a cup of coffee while you dress. So up and at 'em."

Rosie scrambled out of the bed as

soon as the door closed behind him. She used the chamber pot, pulled off her nightgown, grabbed her chemise and corset and got them on with all speed. Then she put on her dusty traveling suit from the day before. No need to dirty another outfit just to sit on a buckboard all day long. She was just putting her nightgown in the valise when he returned with two steaming cups of coffee.

"Here you go," he said, handing her one. "I didn't know how you like it, so it's just black."

"Thanks. Black is fine. Sometimes I put a little milk in it, but normally it's black for me."

"Mary is about ready to serve breakfast. I'll take your bags down to the foyer and we can go eat, then leave for home."

"How long will it be? To get home, I mean." She took a sip of the strong brew, then set it down and began unbraiding her hair.

"It's about two and a half hours to Duncan's. Duncan and Catherine McKenzie are watching my kids for me. We'll have to visit for a bit. Catherine's got a lot of questions for you. She's never met a mail order bride before. Actually, none of us have. You're the first in these parts. Then it's another three hours to my ranch from there. That's why I think you'll barely have time to fix supper before the sun goes down. It'll be four o'clock or after before we get home."

"What about you? Do you have any questions for me?" She ran her fingers through her hair and loosened it before gathering it up into a bun atop her head.

"We'll have a lot of time to talk on the way home. Time enough to get to know each other some."

She glanced over at him, wondering if her fiddling with her hair had worked and he was pleased with what she saw. He looked at her with hunger in his eyes. He was weakening. "Well, I do have a question, just one more for now. Is the bank open yet?"

"No. Why?"

"I didn't want you to worry, but I

brought a bank draft with me that I need to deposit. It's my dowry, in the amount of five thousand dollars. I wasn't going to tell you, in case I needed it to leave, but I'm not going to. I'm determined to make a go of this."

"Five thousand dollars! That's a hell of a lot of money."

"My parents were wealthy. I've been living with my brother until now. The five thousand is all I have in the world. I know it sounds like a lot of money, but it wouldn't take long to go through it if I had to live on it."

He nodded in agreement. "You're right. I'm glad to hear you're determined to make a go of it, but I still don't think you know what you're in for. It's not an easy life on a ranch. You'll have to do the washing, cleaning, cooking. You're expected to gather the eggs and milk the cows. Do you know how to milk a cow?"

She shook her head. What *had* she gotten herself into? Milking cows?

"I'll teach you. It's not hard. Did you

keep chickens in Philadelphia?"

"No. We bought all of our meat and eggs from a butcher or the market each week and kept them in the ice box."

"Well, I'll teach you how to gather eggs, too, so you don't get pecked. The hens don't like to give up their eggs. Is there anything you can do? Besides cook, I mean."

"I know how to clean a house," she said, her feelings bristling. "I'm not completely useless. I can teach your children reading, writing, and arithmetic. *And* I can cook. Whatever else I need to know, I'll learn. I'm a quick study and eager to learn everything I can."

"Eager to learn, huh?" His lip quirked up. "Glad to hear it. You're going to have a lot to learn in a short period of time. Shall we go?" He picked up her bags.

"Yes, but I want to go to the bank first. I've got that draft and I've carried it long enough."

"All right." He checked his pocket

watch. "It's eight thirty. The bank opens at nine. We'll be done with breakfast right about then."

He turned toward the open door and held it for her. "Let's get moving. We've got a long trip ahead of us."

This was her last chance to back out. She actually thought about it, but she wanted a family, and she'd take her chances on changing his mind about wanting more children. If she couldn't, she'd at least have his two to raise as her own.

After breakfast they went to the bank. After that, they'd go out to the McKenzie's where she'd meet Tom's children for the first time.

Her stomach churned. There was bound to be some resentment on their part. After all, in their eyes she was taking their dead mother's place. But she shouldn't be this nervous. She'd talk to Tom on the way there. After all, it was nearly a three hour trip, there would be plenty of time to discuss everything.

The buckboard was tied to the

hitching rail in front of the boardinghouse. Tom placed the bags in the back. That's when she noticed the supplies he had. There looked to be bags of grain, beans, sugar, flour, and coffee. She was especially happy to see a small bag of tea among all the other groceries. Plenty of food stuffs to cook with if she had meat to go with it. He'd gotten cans of fruit, too. Peaches. She could make a cobbler or a pie. Something easy to begin with. Later she could dazzle him with her baking skills. Her brother had loved all the treats she used to bake for him. Perhaps Tom had a sweet tooth. She could use it to soften him up. Her thoughts consumed her as they walked down the street.

Tom stopped in front of the bank. "Before we go in, I want you to know that I don't want your money. It's yours to do with as you please."

She smiled at him. "Thank you. You don't know how much it means to me to hear you say that."

He nodded. "You're welcome."

He held the door for her and then called out to one of the men behind the counter. "Hello, Sam."

The man, short, skinny, and balding, with his graying hair combed over from one side in a fruitless effort to hide the bald spot, looked up. "Well hello, Tom. Is this the new Mrs. Harris?"

"Yes. This is Rosie. Rosie, this is Sam Kent, president of the bank."

Rosie held out her hand. "Pleased to meet you, Mr. Kent."

"And you, Mrs. Harris," he replied. "What can I do for you both today?"

"I need to open an account and deposit a draft from my bank in Philadelphia," said Rosie.

"Certainly, Mrs. Harris. Tom already has an account here, so…"

"No, Mr. Kent, this is my account, not my husband's."

Sam looked over at Tom who nodded. "Very well. Please fill this out." He handed her a form.

It only took her a couple of minutes to complete. "Here you go, Mr. Kent. Also, I would like twenty-five dollars in cash please."

"What do you need cash for?" Tom, suspicious, asked. "Nothing to buy on the ranch and we don't get peddlers. They aren't allowed on my property."

"I want to stop at the mercantile and get a small gift for each of your children." She twisted her hands together, causing her reticule to bounce off her skirt. "I can only imagine what they must be feeling, and perhaps this small token will help ease things between us. I also want to pick up the school supplies they'll need, or perhaps I should say, that are available."

"Are you trying to bribe my children?"

She hesitated for only a moment. "Do you think it will work?"

Tom chuckled. She was amazed at the transformation a simple laugh made in his face. Gone were the hard lines formed from a steady frown. His eyes sparkled and reminded her of sapphires.

"It just might. You never know with kids. Something that works this time won't the next."

Mr. Kent came back to the counter. "Here you go, Mrs. Harris. Here's the receipt for the deposit and twenty-five dollars in cash. Is there anything else I can do for you?"

"No, thank you. I appreciate all your help."

"Goodbye, Sam. See you next time we come to town," Tom said as he placed his hand on her waist. The contact, though slight, sent shivers right through her.

"You bet. See you then."

Tom ushered her out the door and they walked to the mercantile. His hand remained firmly on her waist in a proprietary gesture. She liked it. Liked the feeling of being wanted, even if only for her domestic skills.

Rosie chose a doll for Suzie and a

pocket knife for Ben. Tom assured her they didn't have either of the items.

She also purchased slates, chalk, books on history, mathematics, and spelling for Ben, and a couple of coloring books and colored pencils for Suzie. She asked Sadie, the owner, what books the local school teacher ordered and asked her to order the same ones for her.

"It'll take about a month for them to get here. Hope that's all right," said Sadie.

"I'm not going anywhere, so there's no hurry. This is my home now, and the children need to catch up to their classmates." She said it to Sadie, but it was more for herself than the store's proprietor.

She *was* home. Wasn't she?

CHAPTER 3

They rode in the buckboard for thirty minutes and were a couple of miles from town. The sun beat down and it was hot even though it was only midmorning. Rosie was glad for her bonnet but a parasol would be heaven right now.

Neither one of them had said a thing. It was time to break the ice and start talking.

"Why did you want a mail order bride? Aren't there any single women here?" she asked as she fiddled with the string ties to her reticule. "I know you probably think this is a question asked too late, but I was simply glad for a way out of my current living situation. I had to get away from my sister-in-law."

He nodded in understanding. "There are none that my kids like. None that didn't want more children."

"You said last night you don't want more children? Why?"

"Don't get me wrong. I love my children, but I don't want to get stuck with any more from the next woman who leaves me."

"And you do so much to make a woman want to stay," she said under her breath. "What makes you think I'm going to leave you? I didn't come all this way just to up and leave again," she said loud enough for him to hear.

"Women leave. That's what they do. As soon as someone comes along offering them the moon, they're gone."

"You shouldn't judge all women by your stupid wife. You didn't say anything in your letters about not wanting children." This development saddened her more than she could say. It was one thing to not have a chance at a real marriage. One with love, respect and friendship. But to not have her own children almost too much to take. She bit back a sob and swiped at her eyes. Her entire marriage, her new life was built on a lie. She would not cry.

"Didn't figure I'd get many responses if I mentioned that fact."

"No, you wouldn't have, including mine. Most women want children of their own. What if your kids don't like me?"

"I figure that's going to be up to you. They'll be a tough sell. Ben especially. He was very close to his mother. Suzie, on the other hand, doesn't remember her. She was only a baby, just barely one, when Sarah died."

"I see."

"I don't think you do. I need a cook, housekeeper and mother for my children. That's all. Don't have any illusions about love, Rosie. It won't happen. A woman already betrayed me once. I won't be taken in again. Don't expect love from me."

"So now you feel it's all right to betray me? Why? Because I'm a woman? Not wanting children was not something you ever mentioned in your letters, but I'll try to remember what your feelings are."

"If I recall correctly, you didn't mention it either. That's one of the reasons I chose you. You seemed straightforward and practical without silly, girlish notions."

"I don't think wanting love and children in my life is a girlish notion. But you're right, I don't have any delusions that you may fall in love with me. I gave up on finding love a long time ago. I *was* hoping for friendship."

He was silent. Finally, he asked, "What put you off love, or perhaps I should say who?"

She looked down at her gloved hands clasped in her lap. "I had a beau who I thought cared for me. All he cared for was my money. When he found someone with more, he dropped me like a hot iron."

"I'm sorry, Rosie. That explains some things."

"Like what? *What* can you garner from those few sentences?"

He turned his head and those deep blue eyes bore into her. "I can see why you would answer an advertisement for a mail order bride. You were hurt and looking for someone to validate your existence."

"I don't *need* validation. I was looking for a way to have a home of my own. One I can't be thrown out of. Of course, that has yet to be seen, doesn't it?" She didn't want to talk about this any longer. It was painful enough to know that she wasn't desirable to Tom. "Tell me more about your children," she said, changing the subject.

His features visibly softened at the mention of his children. She saw on his face how much he loved them, and swallowed the lump in her throat.

"I am lucky enough to have two beautiful children. Ben, who's ten, is my serious one. He's a good student, as you'll see. He always has his nose in a book and would rather read than anything."

"I wish you'd told me that before. I'd have gotten him books for his gift."

"You didn't ask what they wanted, only if they would like what you picked out," he said softly.

She let out a sigh. "You're right. All I wanted to know was how old they are. I'm sorry. That was very presumptuous of me."

"It's all right, he'll enjoy the pocket knife, too."

"I did bring a few books with me, maybe he'd like to read them, if he hasn't already."

"I'm sure he will. Giddy up." He slapped the reins on the butts of the team. They were beginning to slow trying to eat the grass along the side of the road.

The country side was beautiful. Unlike anything she'd ever seen before. The mountains stood purple against the blue sky. The grasses were growing and meadows filled with a riot of colors from flowers she couldn't name. Amazing country. Beautiful. Wild.

She itched to get her watercolors out and paint it though she knew the watercolors wouldn't do it justice. Oils would be much better to capture the vibrancy of color all around her.

"You'll have to teach me to drive a team. It doesn't look too hard, but I've never done it and probably should know how."

"You're right, you should." He passed the reins to her. "There's not much to it. If you want to turn left, pull back on the left rein, right on the right rein. To stop or slow down, pull back on both reins at the same time. To get them going, slap them on their rumps, like I just did. You try it."

She took a rein in each hand and slapped them down. It did almost nothing.

"You need to flick it with your wrist. Like this," he put his arm around her then took her hands in his and flicked the reins.

He was so warm, in a way that had nothing to do with the sun and everything to do with his effect on her. She wanted nothing more than to lean into him and draw his warmth to her. Glancing up, she found him gazing at her. She swallowed hard and lowered her eyes back to the horses.

His hands lingered on hers for an extra moment, at least she thought they did, before he leaned back to his side of the bench.

He cleared his throat. "Well, you see what I mean."

Breathless from just his touch, she felt heat in her cheeks. "Yes, I do. I imagine it would be a little different with a lighter vehicle, like a buggy. The horses wouldn't want to go so slow and they'd be harder to control."

He nodded.

Her breathing back under control, she tried for the mundane. A safe subject. "So, what about Suzie? She's three now, correct?"

"Yes. She was just a baby when Sarah left, so she doesn't remember her at all. Suzie was our surprise baby. After so many years, we thought Ben would be our only child. Then Sarah got pregnant with Suzie. I thought she doted on both kids. Her bond with Ben seemed special, just as mine is with Suzie. That little one has me wrapped around her finger and she knows it. She's my ornery one."

"How did you manage a baby all alone after she was gone?"

"My mother's a widow and came to help me. But she had to leave to help her sister, and she thought it was time I married again anyway."

"So, you placed an ad and got me. I bet you got lots of responses. What made you choose mine?"

"You were the only one who sent a photograph."

"Oh." Well, that was something, and she felt a little better. Actually, she decided he must have found her pleasing enough. He'd sent for her, hadn't he? Maybe seducing him would be easier than she thought.

She smiled.

*****

Tom knew he'd hurt her again. He didn't do it on purpose, but for some reason, everything he said came out wrong. Though he wanted her to know where he stood, he didn't want her to take it as personal. He would have done the same thing no matter who it was that he'd picked.

He'd picked her because she was pretty in her photograph. He'd lied when he said she was the only one who sent one. Several of the other women had, but Rosie's was the one he kept coming back to. The one he thought about during the day, and looked at before bed at night.

Even under the dirt, soot and grime from the trip, he could see her beauty. He was scared. Everyone left. He knew that. He no longer had the same innocence of commitment, so he decided looks were paramount. He picked her.

He'd chosen correctly. In person, she was spectacular.

*****

They arrived at the McKenzie's right around noon. Ben came running out, Suzie followed as fast as her chubby little legs would carry her. "Papa," yelled Ben, as he ran down the porch steps.

Tom helped Rosie down, and then turned just as Ben hurtled into his side. Suzie launched herself at Tom completely confident he would catch her, which he did. He stood there holding both of his children. "Kids, this is Rosie. She's your new mother. Say hello."

Ben stepped away from his father and held out his hand. He was a little sullen, but obedient to what his father expected him to do. "Hello, I'm Ben."

The perfect little gentleman, Tom beamed with pride in his son.

"Hello, Ben. I know you already have a mother, and I'm not trying to take her place, so I would be pleased if you could call me Rosie."

Ben perked up a bit. "Alright, Rosie."

"Suzie," prompted her father. "What

do you say?"

She took her thumb out of her mouth. "Hello."

Suzie tried to put her thumb back in her mouth, but Tom stopped her and shook his head.

Suzie sighed and dropped her hand. "Sorry, Papa."

"It's all right. Mama will help us remember, too, from now on. Won't you, Mama?" said Tom.

Rosie nodded, unable for the moment to say anything. Mama. The one word she'd waited all her life to hear. "Of course, I will."

A beautiful red-haired woman carrying a baby, and one of the most handsome men Rosie had ever seen, followed Tom's children down the stairs. With them was a boy about four.

"Catherine and Duncan McKenzie, this is my wife Rosie."

"Hello, pleased to make your

acquaintance," said Rosie.

"It's always so good to have another woman in the valley. We are few and far between. Now come on in, and of course, you'll stay for dinner. We've plenty and I've got so many questions for you, Rosie," said Catherine.

Rosie laughed. "Tom said you would. I'm somewhat of an oddity. I guess there aren't too many mail order brides in 1890. Not like thirty years ago."

Catherine ushered them all into the kitchen where some of their dinner was already on the table. Wonderful smells wafted under her nose. Chicken, mashed potatoes and gravy sat on the stove on the warming shelf. Her mouth watered. She hadn't realized, until she'd seen all the food how hungry she was. Normally a good eater, she'd picked at her breakfast at Mary's. Nerves. Anxious about meeting Tom's children she was sure.

"Is there anything I can do?" asked Rosie.

"Not a thing. You just sit and relax.

It's probably been a stressful few weeks for you. Leaving everything you know, traveling to a new place, and marrying a virtual stranger. That would take a lot out of anybody. Would you care to freshen up?" Catherine said while she put the food on the table, looking over Rosie's travel-weary attire.

"I'd love it. It was a difficult trip. Sleeping in a bed last night was a luxury after sleeping sitting up for the last five nights."

"That's a long trip. There's a basin with water and towels right there at the sink."

"It definitely is not a trip for the timid. I had to wait for the train at several different depots and, in Denver, I had to stay overnight in the station in order to catch the train coming here. I changed trains again in Alamosa to get the one to Creede. This place is sort of out of the way," Rosie said as she walked to the kitchen sink.

"I hadn't realized the trip would be so difficult. You're probably exhausted. I'm sorry, I should have let you rest another day at the boardinghouse," said Tom as he sat at the table with Duncan.

"Don't be ridiculous. I'm anxious to see my new home and couldn't wait to meet the children."

"Why'd you want to meet us, Mama?" asked Suzie.

Rosie's heart clenched when Suzie called her Mama. Somehow having the child say it made it all that much sweeter. She finished drying her hands and walked over to Suzie, who sat on her daddy's lap. Bending down so she was eye level with Suzie, she said, "Well, if I'm going to be your mama and help your papa take care of you, I wanted to know who you are."

"So you gonna care for us now?"

"Yes, sugar, I'm going to care for you now."

"I'm not sugar. I'm Suzie."

"So you are. You're just so sweet, I thought for a minute you were sugar," laughed Rosie.

Suzie smiled and buried her face in her father's neck. Though still shy, Rosie thought she'd made a friend in Suzie. Ben was a different matter. He was polite but reserved. He didn't join in any of the conversation, but rather stared at Rosie.

Finally, she looked over at Ben. "You're awfully quiet, Master Ben. What's on your mind?"

"Nuttin'."

"Nothing."

"That's what I said."

"No, you said nuttin', which is not a word."

He looked over at his father, fury on his face. "May I be excused?"

"After you say it correctly, then you may be excused."

"Nothing." Ben stood and ran from the room.

"I'm afraid I blundered," said Rosie. Embarrassed as much as Ben must have been. "I shouldn't have corrected him."

"No, he needs to be corrected when he is wrong. Perhaps it was the wrong time, since we're not at home."

Rosie blushed. "You're absolutely right. Excuse me, I need to find Ben and apologize."

"He's probably out in the barn. One of the cats had a litter of kittens about three weeks ago. The kids have terrorized the poor things with their enthusiasm," said Duncan.

She went out to the barn. Sure enough, Ben was there, sitting on the ground with several kittens crawling all over him.

"Ben, may I sit?" She didn't really want to, the barn smelled and she was sure there were all kinds of feces in the straw, but she needed to win him over, and it wasn't like it would be at all noticeable on her grimy travel clothes.

"Do what you want."

She sat down and picked up one of the kittens to keep her hands busy. It

immediately mewled at her. "Ben, I'm sorry.
I should never have corrected you in front of
your friends."

"You embarrassed me," he blurted.

"I know and I'm sorry. Will you
forgive me?"

He rolled one of the kittens over onto
its back and tickled its belly. It fought back,
biting and bucking the hand that held it. If
she hadn't been there, she was sure he'd be
laughing at the little tiger's antics.

"I guess so," he said, still sullen.

Rosie almost laughed. His pout was
so pronounced and she could tell he was
having a hard time maintaining it.

"Thank you. I understand you like to
read. I have some books with me that you
might like. They're by Jules Verne, and are
wonderful stories of adventure."

Ben's eyes lit up.

"They're some of my favorites. I have
Around the World in Eighty Days, Journey
to the Center of the Earth, and Twenty

Thousand Leagues Under the Sea. Do you like adventure stories?"

"More than anything. Could I read one of them tonight?"

"If it's all right with your father, it's fine with me. Which one would you like first?"

"I think Twenty Thousand Leagues Under the Sea. I've never seen the ocean."

"All right. Remind me after we get home and I'll dig it out of my traveling bags."

Ben beamed. Rosie thought she might have made some headway. At least for tonight.

CHAPTER 4

Tom was right. According to her pin watch, it was four-fifteen when they arrived at the ranch. He pulled the buckboard to a stop along the front of the house. Around the side she saw what she thought was probably the kitchen. Laundry tubs and a small table with a bucket and basin on it sat on the large covered porch just outside the side door.

Painted white, the two story house had another covered porch off the front. She pictured Tom and herself sitting in the rocking chairs, watching the sun set. Or sitting in the swing, quietly talking after the children were in bed.

Large picture windows faced the

mountains. It must have cost a fortune to ship in that much glass. Rosie guessed they were in the parlor. She would open the curtains to let in the natural light and have indoor plants in front of the windows. Maybe some of the wild flowers from the fields they'd passed. Assuming that Tom let her make any changes to the décor.

Behind the main house stood the rest of the buildings. First the pump house with a small windmill turning in the light and welcome breeze. Followed by the ice house and chicken coop, then the bunkhouse and a privy. If that was the only privy, it would be a long walk to get to it. Quite a distance beyond the bunkhouse was the barn where, presumably, the milk cows were kept. Rosie was not looking forward to tomorrow. It would be a long day, learning how to milk a cow and gather eggs, besides cooking all the meals. Oh, for the conveniences of Philadelphia!

Ben scrambled down from the wagon as soon as it stopped and reached up to get his sister. Tom came around to Rosie's side to help her. She placed her hands on his broad shoulders while he gripped her waist and lifted her easily to the ground. Her heart sped up when he touched her, and she noticed her breathing was a little labored. All from one simple touch. What in the world would she do if…no *when*…he made love to her?

Tom grabbed her valises from the back of the wagon and went up the stairs into the house. Rosie picked up her skirts and scrambled after him. When she entered the house, the stairway was right in front of her with a hallway to the right. She would have to explore those rooms later. Tom took the stairs two at a time and Rosie ran to catch up. At the top of the stairs, he stopped and waited for her.

"Sorry. I forgot you were behind me. Down this hall are the bedrooms and the bathroom."

Rosie stopped. "Did you say bathroom? With running water and everything?" She envisioned a hot bath. A long, hot soak.

"Yes. We're the first in the valley to have indoor plumbing. It was something I did to make Sarah happy. At least I thought she was happy." He stopped at a door on the right side at the end of the hall, opened it and stepped back, letting her look in. It was the bathroom. With a large, claw-footed tub, a toilet with tank hanging on the wall above the bowl, and a small sink. She was in heaven.

"There's a boiler outside. That's one of your jobs, to make sure that boiler has coal. Coal runs hotter and lasts longer than wood, although we use wood when we run out of coal. I get a wagon load once a month and put it in the coal shed next to the boiler. You'll have to stoke it every morning. We use wood in the fireplaces and coal in the cook stove."

"Am I expected to chop the wood?" The more she learned about all the chores she was expected to do, the more she decided he wanted a slave, not a wife.

He looked her up and down, apparently finding her lacking, thank goodness, before he answered. "No, I'll chop the wood for you. You're going to be plenty busy as it is."

"Speaking of which, I'm sure the

children are hungry. I should start supper. Can you show me to the kitchen?"

"Right. The kitchen is directly below us and also has hot and cold running water. Couldn't see the point of putting it in the bathroom and not the kitchen. Might as well do it all at once. Took nearly six months to install everything, but it was worth it to see Sarah's face when it was done."

Rosie walked beside him down the hall, then behind him down the stairs. "Tell me about your wife. What happened?"

Tom stopped abruptly and rounded on her. "She left me and then she died. That's all you need to know."

Rosie felt like she'd been slapped. Again. She'd never had anyone talk to her with such vehemence in his voice, but she stood her ground. "I…I only thought I might help the children if I knew more about their mother. Your whole point of bringing me out here for this farce of a marriage was to have someone to take care of them. So give me the tools I need to do that."

Tom wiped his face with both hands,

clearly as tired as she was. She was dead on her feet. The trip had taken its toll. Her feet were swollen and achy. Her eyes felt like they had sand in them, and her back was stiff from the ride in the buckboard. All she wanted to do was take her damn corset off and get into a hot tub, but that would have to wait. Getting supper on was her first priority.

"I'm sorry. I shouldn't have..." he said.

She raised her hand and shook her head. "Now I know exactly where you stand. Just show me to the kitchen so I can get one of my chores for the evening done. I won't forget why you brought me here."

"Rosie, I..."

She shook her head. Her vision blurred by unshed tears. She was tired. It had been a long week, she needed rest and there wouldn't be any of that coming anytime soon.

He took a deep breath, turned and continued to the kitchen, in the back of the house. They passed the parlor and the dining room on their way there. The kitchen was large and square. On the wall across the room from them were the sink and icebox with counters in between. There were more cupboards and counter space on the wall with the door to the covered porch. Along the third wall was the doorway where they stood, and a huge buffet and hutch with what appeared to be fine china in it. The last wall had the stove and a door to what she assumed was the pantry. In the middle of the kitchen stood a large table with benches on either side and a chair with arm rests at either end.

"I better get cooking. Did you say there would be fifteen for supper?"

"Yes. I'm sure the ranch hands will be starving after eating Orvie's cooking for two days."

"Then you'd best go and let me get started." She didn't wait for him to leave, but went directly to the icebox to see what was available. She found three chickens ready to be cut up for the fryer. She figured Orvie must have prepared them not knowing when Tom would return. In the pantry she found potatoes, canned peas, and the makings for biscuits. She also found two tins of peaches that she could use for a cobbler.

Two and a half hours later, she had all the food on the table and went to find Tom. She found Ben first and asked him if he would tell his father supper was ready.

"You just need to bang the triangle. Come on, I'll show you."

He walked out to the porch off the kitchen where she saw the large triangle hanging from the ceiling near the edge of the porch. There was a rod attached to it. Rosie took the rod and ran it around the inside. The noise was deafening but effective. Within five minutes, all the men, including Tom, were either on the porch washing up with the soap, basin and towels she'd put out for that purpose, or sitting at the table, waiting for her to sit before loading up their plates. She was surprised and pleased at the restraint and courtesy they showed her.

"Men," said Tom, "this is my wife, Rosie. You'll extend her all the respect due her as my wife."

"Nice to meet you, Rosie," they all said at once. "I'm Joe…" "I'm Bill…" and on around the table it went until all eleven of the men had introduced themselves.

"I'm happy to meet you all. I'd love it if you would give me some ideas of what you like to eat, I'll see about accommodating you. Just don't give them to me all at once. I need to be able to write them down."

They nodded in agreement.

Rosie noticed Tom stared at her while she talked with his men. She felt her color rise and was sure she'd done something wrong, but couldn't think what. Maybe she wasn't supposed to ask the men what they liked to eat. But it would help her with menus if she knew what people wanted. She intended to get the same information from Tom and the children.

Tom drew her attention like a magnet. She couldn't stop herself from glancing up at him every few minutes. The conversations going on around the table faded to the background. Tom sat at the end of the table directly across from her. Too far away to talk to.

She picked at her supper. All the men said it was delicious, so she was gratified. The things Tom said kept running through her mind, over and over again, like they were lines in a play she was supposed to memorize.

I don't need a woman. Been betrayed. Won't do it again. Don't want more children.

That last one, the kicker. Rosie had to change his mind. She would never be happy in a marriage without children. Yes, she had two, but she wanted more. Glancing up, she saw Tom was staring at her again. Something in his eyes gave her hope. The look told her he wasn't as indifferent to her as he said he was.

Me thinks he doth protest too much, as the Bard would say, thought Rosie. She started planning her campaign to make her marriage real in all respects.

Later, when the men were filing out of the kitchen, their bellies full, she worked her way around the table and sat by Tom. "I brought some books and, with your permission, I'd like to let Ben start reading one tonight."

Tom looked over at Ben, who was pleading with his eyes. Rosie watched father and son, and couldn't help but smile. Both were so alike with their dark hair and blue eyes. Ben would to be a heartbreaker, if his father was any indication.

Finally, Tom answered, "I don't see why he shouldn't be able to start a new book tonight. Lord knows he's read everything in this house at least twice."

"With your permission," she glanced up at Tom, "I'd like to send for my books. My brother can ship them to me. I have a good amount, as I'm an avid reader myself. I could put them in the parlor, if you'd build some bookshelves."

"Can she, Papa, please?"

"Sure. But I won't be able to build you the bookcases anytime soon. We're going to start branding soon. I'll be too busy to build shelves. After that's done, I'll get the lumber. Oh, and I'll have a few extra men coming on for the season. They'll be here to help with the branding and then with taking the herd up to summer pasture."

"Will you go with them?" asked Rosie innocently.

"Trying to get rid of me already?"

"No, of course not, I just…"

Tom laughed. She liked the rich baritone sound. He was teasing her. She liked that, too.

CHAPTER 5

After supper, Rosie made Ben wash up before bed. She wanted him to take a bath, but he balked and, considering their tentative truce, she agreed to just let him wash his face and hands and brush his teeth. Then she went upstairs and retrieved the book she'd promised him. He snatched it from her hands with a quick thank you, sat in front of the fire and started reading.

Rosie went back to the kitchen and did the dishes before getting Suzie for her bath. The little girl splashed and played, getting Rosie almost as wet as she was.

Finally, both children were in bed. Now Rosie had to face time alone with Tom. Why did her heart race and her mouth become dry as dust? She'd spent time alone with Tom before. But that was before she saw the look of need in his eyes. Tonight she'd start her campaign to get him to change his mind about having a real marriage, one where he'd make love to her and she might have children.

He sat in one of the comfortable overstuffed chairs in front of the fireplace in the parlor. Rosie went over and sat in the chair beside his.

"You did fine on your first day. Supper was delicious, especially the peach cobbler with fresh cream," said Tom, as he looked into the fire. He seemed lost as to what to say.

"Thank you. I'm glad you enjoyed it. I think I'll make tea. Would you like some?"

"No, but I'll take a cup of coffee if we have any."

Rosie got up from her chair. "We do, and I believe it's still warm."

She came back with the drinks. "So, what are my chores tomorrow? Will you take me through them the first time? I already know I'll need to milk the cows and gather eggs."

"Yes, those are done first thing. Then you make breakfast. Afterwards, there are dishes, and tomorrow is laundry day. Sarah always did laundry on Saturday. The tubs are outside the kitchen and the buckets for filling them are on the porch."

She sipped her tea, holding it with both hands so he wouldn't see them shake.

"In the afternoon, if you get the laundry done, you can teach the children. Oh, and you'll have to watch Suzie a bit. She still tries to get into things, as three-year-olds are want to do."

"I'm sure she does." She smiled and shook her head. "She's quite the little pistol."

He chuckled. "The secret is out. Suzie actually runs the place. Ben and I are at her mercy."

"Well, that's going to change. Suzie must learn boundaries. Both her own and ours. Is that going to be a problem? She's not going to be happy about it, but she's only three." Rosie sipped her tea.

Tom sobered and looked over at Rosie. "If you can get her to behave, I'd be grateful. I haven't had the heart to do much in the way of discipline, and I know I've let Ben get away with more than I ought. He was so close to his mother and was devastated when she left. He's the one who's been watching over Suzie. You may have more of a problem with him than with her, when it comes to teaching her to behave."

"Well, tomorrow is going to come early, and it sounds like I have my work cut out for me. I think I'll turn in."

He nodded. "I'll be up after I finish my coffee."

"Fine. Goodnight."

Rosie went up the stairs to the bedroom. She'd been so busy since they got home, she hadn't even put her clothes away. Her valises were just where Tom had left them. She opened drawers in the bureau hoping to find room for her things. She found that Tom had cleared out a couple of drawers and part of the wardrobe for her. She was touched that he would think of her needs. Maybe there was hope after all. She would use the small gesture to fortify her during his belligerent times which she was afraid might be many. She opened one of her valises and unpacked it into the drawers.

Even as rude as he was, Rosie couldn't imagine leaving him if he loved her. Obviously he'd loved his wife, or he wouldn't be so upset after all this time, would he? She didn't know. All she knew is she needed to get a move on, if she wanted to have her unpacking done before he came up to the bedroom.

Both valises were emptied and slid them under the bed for storage. Unbuttoning her blouse, she peeled the sleeves down her arms and took it off, letting it hit the floor. Then she undid her skirt and it followed the blouse. It was a good thing tomorrow was laundry day, her blouse needed a good scrubbing, as did her skirt. She'd have to brush her jacket and get as much of the dust out of it as she could. As she unfastened her corset, she heard the door open and turned to find Tom staring at her.

"Well come in and close the door," she said as she continued to unlace her corset.

She had on her chemise underneath, so it wasn't like she was naked. Though from the look on Tom's face, she might as well have been. Rosie wasn't experienced, but even she recognized the look as one of pure lust. Time to put her plan in motion.

"I'm glad you're here. I can't seem to get this lace undone. Will you help me, please?"

He didn't say anything but moved forward like he was made of wood. Her corset laced up the front so she could get in and out of it without a maid, but he wouldn't know that. She turned to face him. She'd unlaced it from the bottom up especially for this occasion. Then she knotted the silk laces just below her breasts, so he would have to help her and brush up against her breasts to undo the laces.

Raising her arms, she began taking out the pins that held her hair in its bun on top of her head. It also had the side effect of raising her breasts and thrusting them forward. Quite nicely, she thought.

She watched his hands shake and he took a deep breath before he took a hold of her corset and undid the knot. Proof positive he wasn't immune to her.

Her breasts spilled into his hands as he opened the top lace and the corset fell to the floor. When their skin touched, she couldn't help herself and took a sharp breath, at this his eyes opened and their gazes met. Something passed between them and his hands turned and caressed her plump breasts. His thumbs teased her nipples through the fine fabric of her chemise, until they were hard little points.

Rosie let her unpinned hair tumble free and grasped Tom's shoulders for support. Then she moaned with pleasure as his thumbs worked their magic. Her moan broke the spell. Tom's eyes opened and their gazes met again, both full of need. He pulled his hands away from her.

"You tempt me, woman, more than I thought possible, but I won't change my mind."

He turned his back on her and left the room.

"Well, that went well," she said to herself. She shook out her hair and began to brush it. "I won't give up on you, Tom. I won't. You're my husband and I will have a real marriage," she vowed aloud to his fading footsteps, not caring if he heard. Now that he'd left, her breathing began to return to normal. She fanned herself. Lord, it was hot in here.

*****

Tom poured three fingers of whiskey in a glass and drank it down. Then he poured three more. What the hell had come over him? Didn't he remember what Sarah did to him? Women weren't to be trusted. A little voice inside him spoke up. *But Rosie's different. Rosie is nothing like Sarah.*

The voice was right. Sarah was never happy living on the ranch. She didn't like the work, didn't like the house and, apparently, didn't like him or the kids either. But Rosie…Rosie *was* different. She had her own money and still came. She didn't have to tell him about the money, but she did. Even after learning about all the chores he had for her, she stayed. Rosie liked his kids, was already thinking about them and their needs for the future before she'd even met them.

Ben already liked her. She brought him books. Tom loved the fact that he cherished reading. Sarah never could relate to that. She wasn't a reader and couldn't understand her husband and son's interest in it.

No, Rosie was light to Sarah's dark, but did that mean he could trust her? It was too soon. He'd only known her for two days. No, that wasn't exactly true. He knew her through her letters.

They'd exchanged several letters before he'd finally asked her to marry him. There were other responses to his advertisement, but none stood out like Rosie's. Her letters always gave him a smile, whether she was relating some atrocious thing her new sister-in-law had done, or telling him about the neighbor's new puppy.

Then she'd sent a photograph. He'd actually fallen a bit more under her spell with the picture. He saw her full lips and clear eyes. He saw her light hair, but hadn't expected it to be as lovely as it was.

Even covered in dirt and grime from the trip, she'd been stunning. And then at Mary's, when she'd finally been able to wash her face, he'd been awestruck by her simple beauty. Her pale skin, unblemished, her dark brown eyes, pools of brandy on a perfect canvas. And her lips. Full, red, ideal for kisses. His kisses.

All of it made him more determined than ever to keep her at a distance. She didn't care for that idea. Her ingenuity at finding ways to have him touch her made him smile, and also sent him flying down here for a whiskey or two.

He had to keep her at arms' length, but how was he supposed to do that when he slept with her every night? How was he going to keep his traitorous subconscious from making love to her? That was the real question. He was afraid he'd wake to find her under him, moaning in pleasure, much as she'd done tonight.

She did have the most beautiful breasts. High and round, they filled his hands perfectly. And her skin. Had he ever seen anyone with skin so soft and flawless? How he wanted to take her pert nipple into his mouth and suck until she begged him to take her. Her moan was the only thing that saved him this time.

No way in hell he was going to be put in a position where he could be betrayed again. The kids were the only thing that kept him sane last time. They needed him. He couldn't wallow in self-pity, he'd had to care for his children. They didn't know anything except Mama was gone. Ben understood now that his mother was dead, but Suzie didn't. Her grandma was the only 'mother' she'd known, and now Rosie would be her mother. But that was all she'd be. A mother for his children. Nothing more.

Suzie already seemed to like Rosie. She'd been ecstatic when she'd received Rosie's gift of a new doll. Wouldn't let it out of her sight. Insisted on taking it to bed with her.

And Ben. When he found out Rosie liked to read, she'd become his best friend. Someone he could share his love of books with. His kids needed Rosie and all the beauty she brought with her. *They* needed her. He didn't.

Even the men seemed to like Rosie. They'd never had anyone ask them what they wanted or liked to eat. They were lucky if Sarah put something on the table that was edible. Her lack of cooking skills were what made him hire the first of many women to help her take care of the house.

Rosie won over everyone just by being herself. Including him if he were to admit it. But he wouldn't be won over. She was nice and pretty, and all the things a wife and mother should be, but he'd made a mistake once and damned if he'd do it again over a pretty face and tempting flesh. And Lord, was she tempting.

Sarah left him for a traveling peddler who promised her the moon and all the stars. The fancy life of ease she'd always wanted. She'd been surprised when they married, to discover she was expected to work. Apparently, she'd never done so before. Just how she got on, he wasn't sure, but after their wedding night and discovering she wasn't the virgin she professed to be, he had a clue. When Ben came along six weeks early, he'd had another. But none of it mattered to him at the time, and only now made him wonder if he was right in thinking she was pregnant when they married. But Ben looked just like him. Right down to the dark hair and blue eyes.

*****

She read the letter again.

Tom Harris remarried. She's rich. Deposited $5000 in bank. Come home, we can make a killing.

All my love,

Your brother.

Folding the letter carefully, she placed it back in the envelope. Things hadn't worked out like she planned, or like Frank promised. Five thousand would get her back to the life of ease, back to the life she wanted. Now she just had to figure out how to get it.

*****

Tom walked into the pen where the chickens were kept and headed for the coop, which was what he called the small shed inside the pen. Rosie followed him. He ignored the chickens and they flapped to get out of his way.

Once inside the chicken coop, he walked behind the nest shelves. There were three shelves in the coop with four nests on each shelf. Not all of them were empty of hens. Those that were, he just plucked the egg from the nest and placed it in the basket he carried. For those that the hen was still there sitting on her egg, he tried first reaching under the sitting hen. If that didn't work, he would push the hen out of the nest and grab the egg.

He held the basket out to her. She took it and went to the next nest. She gingerly reached under the hen and tried to grab the egg. The hen turned and pecked her hand.

"Ow. Why didn't they do that to you?" she said, snatching her hand back and checking for blood.

"Because I'm quicker than you are. Don't be slow and try to take it easy on the hen. They'll peck you every time. Push the hen aside and take the egg. Try it again."

This time she drove her hand under the back end of the chicken, grabbed the egg and was out before the chicken knew what she was up to. She turned grinning toward Tom and showed him her prize.

He smiled back. "Easy, huh?"

"Yes, it is easy." Something pecked her leg. "What in the heck?"

She looked down and the rooster was pecking at her skirt. Hard. She kicked at it and he flapped away.

"That's Walt, my cock."

She raised her eyebrows at him and burst out laughing.

"My rooster."

She nodded, chuckling under her breath.

"You have to watch out for him. He'll peck you every time, if you don't get in and out of here fast. Sometimes feeding them by throwing corn in the yard will distract him enough that you can get in and out without being attacked. Luckily you have your skirt to protect you. Watch it when you go into the coop though. If you don't see him in the yard, he could be in the coop and he won't hesitate to leap at you. He doesn't realize he can't fly."

"I'll remember. I noticed there are only twelve nests, but you have a lot more chickens than that."

"There are only twelve laying hens. The rest we eat. You'll have to do that, too."

"Do what, too?"

"Slaughter the chickens when you need them for a meal."

"I'm not slaughtering any chicken."

"You will if you want to eat them."

"Then you best like beef and pork, because I'm not slaughtering any chicken. Don't know how and don't want to learn." She crossed her arms over her chest.

Tom stared at her for a long moment then grinned. "I like beef and pork. If I want chicken, I'll get Orvie to slaughter them. Fair enough?"

She nodded. "Yes, thank you."

"Did you notice the bin on the side of the coop?"

"Not really. But I do now that you point it out. What's it for?"

"That's where we keep the feed. You'll put three of the cans full around the ground, like this." He filled the can with grain and flung it around the yard and then handed her the can. "Okay, you try it."

She did just like he had done and was inordinately pleased that she'd done it right.

"Great. You have the chickens down pat. Now for the cows."

"Cows?"

"Milking and feeding the cows."

"Oh, yeah. Well, let's get at it."

She followed him to the barn.

CHAPTER 6

The next day, Rosie started with the cows first, before breakfast. It was her first day doing chores alone. Tom went through everything she was supposed to do and showed her how to do them. It took her much longer than it did him to milk the cows. She kept pulling and got nothing. Unfortunately, she was not getting anything. She was using just two fingers to pull, afraid she'd hurt the cow, yet she knew that if she didn't get the milk out, the cow would really be in pain. She started to panic and finally remembered that Tom had used his whole hand. He'd been so good at it, he could squirt the cat in the face with the teat.

She tried again, using all her fingers

and thumb like she remembered him doing. Still not much. Then she remembered he'd sort of punched the udders to get them started. Not hard, just a solid nudging.

After she nudged the udder, she pulled down on the teat and lo and behold! milk squirted out. She did it with the other hand and the same thing happened. Woohoo!! She was milking the cow.

After she got done with the cows, she took the milk to the kitchen where she still had to put it through the cheesecloth and strain it, then separate it into the jugs and put it into the ice house. Once she'd done that, she was ready for a break, but had to gather the eggs and feed the chickens first, and then had to make breakfast.

She went out to the chicken coop. The rooster charged her as soon as she opened the gate. She still felt the peck from yesterday. He'd gotten her good, more so than she let on to Tom.

Today she kicked at him, but he moved too fast. He followed her into the coop and, as soon as she started gathering the eggs, he started pecking her. She went out into the yard and threw some corn around the yard, hoping to distract him while she gathered the eggs. She wasn't that lucky. He stayed in the coop and was lying in wait for her.

Rosie took a deep breath and steeled herself before entering the coop again. She was prepared for the little bastard. He waited on the upper level of the coop, though how he got there, she didn't know. As soon as he saw Rosie, he sailed down directly at her. She took the basket in her hands and batted him away. He hit the wall and was a little dazed, but got back up quickly. A little wobbly, he walked out of the coup looking like he'd had a few too many drinks.

She hadn't meant to hit him hard. Didn't want to injure him, just keep him away from her, so she was glad to see that he was back to normal when she came out of the coop. He charged her, like always, but stopped just short of actually hitting her. So she got lucky and it worked. He was afraid enough of her to stay away. At least for now.

It took Rosie almost all day to milk

and feed the cows, gather the eggs, feed the chickens, and fix the meals. And then today, she still had to do laundry. She'd been able to put it off for one day because Tom had to teach her how to do the rest of the chores, but she couldn't put it off any longer. It made for a very long and tiring day. She boiled the water on the stove, and as it got hotter it got the clothes cleaner. She tried to use the water from the faucets at the sink, but the boiler wasn't that big and she ran it dry in no time. She stirred the laundry in boiling water with a large paddle, used the washboard to scrub each piece of clothing with homemade lye soap, then used a wringer attached to the tub to get the water out. She rinsed in cold water. It seemed to get rid of the soap better and it was easier on her hands than the hot water.

She looked down at her poor hands. They were red and cracked and this was only the second day of chores, and the first time doing the laundry. Another week of this and they'd be bleeding if she hadn't had her cream. She was going to have to get Sadie down at the mercantile to order the rose cream she used on her hands by the gallon. Between the laundry and scrubbing the house, her hands were a wreck.

Tired. Lord, she was tired. Her first laundry day wore her out completely. She'd put the kids to bed and then collapsed in bed herself.

Now that she'd learned how to do everything, she was back to Saturdays being laundry day. Sunday was a day of rest. For everyone except Rosie. She still had to do all the meals and her other chores, which on Sunday included the ironing.

And so it went day after day, week after week, until she realized she'd been there a month. Sure she'd get used to it, but she was surprised when even after a month, she was still exhausted every night. It seemed like she forever fell behind. Never enough time to finish everything, and goodness knows never enough rest.

There were some things she found ways to improve. For instance, she discovered that while cooking, she could do lessons with the kids at the same time. She'd have Ben write down a passage from the book he currently read, then read it out loud to her, and together they identified the parts of the sentence. After that, she gave him equations to do in arithmetic. For Suzie, she'd started teaching her her letters. She was only three after all. Mostly she just drew pictures on the slate while Ben did his work.

Even on Sundays, she quizzed the children.

"Ben, tell me about the book you're reading," Rosie said as she checked the iron to see if it was hot enough. She sprinkled the shirt with water from a small mason jar with tiny holes poked in the lid.

"Well, I'm reading about Captain Nemo and his ship the Nautilus."

"Yes, go on," she said, as she ironed one of Tom's shirts.

"The Nautilus is a really special ship. It can go under the water. Can you imagine?"

Rosie smiled. "What do you imagine?"

"Well, I figure there must be all kind

of wonders. Different kinds of fish and animals. It says they farm seaweed and use it for food. What do you think it tastes like?"

"Suzie, sweetheart, don't eat the chalk. It's for drawing," she said, as Suzie looked up guiltily. "I'm sorry Ben, what about seaweed?"

"Just that I wondered what it would taste like?"

"I think it would be very salty, because it's in the ocean and the ocean is salty. What else might it be like?"

"Well, it's green, so maybe like turnip greens?"

"Good. You're thinking, following a logical step based on its color. I've seen it. It looks a lot like giant blades of grass, but is much darker in color. My brother, Robert, took me to the seashore in New Jersey once. Some seaweed had washed up on the shore. The piece I saw was about a foot wide and three feet long. Robert said it was only a quarter of the fully grown plant."

"Wow. That's big. Rosie, is your

brother our uncle, since you married Papa?"

"Yes, I guess he is. I'll have to write him and let him know that he has a wonderful nephew and niece." *What will Robert think about that? Maybe they could come out here to meet them.* "Now we know that the seaweed is big. Just how big is it if one quarter of its height is three feet?"

Ben thought about it for a moment then took out his slate and wrote it out. "Well, three feet divided by one quarter equals…no, three feet time four equals twelve feet."

"That's right. Very good," praised Rosie. "You're doing great with your numbers."

She finished the shirt, hung it up and started another while the iron was still hot.

Ben beamed with pride.

"That's great, son," Tom said from the doorway to the outside.

"Papa, you were listening?"

"From the seaweed farming on."

"Do you agree with us on how seaweed would taste?"

"I do. It seems reasonable to me. I don't know that I would want to try it. Give me steak and potatoes any day."

"Speaking of food," said Rosie as she continued to iron. "We need supplies. My stores of flour and sugar are sorely depleted, and since we didn't go to town yesterday, I'd like to go tomorrow."

Tom nodded. "I'll arrange for someone to take you."

"No need. I can drive the team myself, and Sadie's husband, Gordon, will load the wagon for me."

"Are you sure you can handle the team? It will be your first time for such a long distance."

She set the iron on the stove to heat up again. "I'll be fine. It's time for me to do it alone."

"You're right. Leave early so you're back before sunset."

"I will. Don't worry."

Rosie got up two hours before sunrise. She hurried through her morning chores, the lantern in her hand shedding light on the path in front of her.

For breakfast, she made fried steak, bacon and sausage, scrambled eggs, fresh biscuits with butter and chokecherry jelly. She had four pies she'd baked last night, and she set out two for breakfast. The rest she put on the warming shelf on the stove so it would still be hot when the men came in.

Then she started lunch. Along with the pinto beans she'd been soaking overnight, she made a stew. She flavored the beans with a couple of ham hocks. She baked more biscuits, some corn bread, and put out two loaves of bread and the other two pies.

The men worked hard and ate great quantities of food to sustain them. Not one of them was fat. All were lean and muscular like Tom. Rosie was hard pressed to cook enough food at every meal to satisfy their needs. She baked twenty loaves of bread every week; made fresh biscuits with every meal. There was always a couple of pies or cakes or cobblers to supplement every meal. She kept a pot of stew or beans going all the time so whenever the men got hungry, there would be something for them to eat.

Because she would be gone for the noon meal, Orvie would cook the main part of it. This included the meat, today fried steak and roasted pork. Some kind of potato, fresh vegetables, if there were any in the garden, but knowing Orvie, he'll just pull some canned goods out of the pantry, rather than go look in the garden for fresh ones.

At the last minute, Tom said, "I remembered things I need to get, too. So I'm going with you."

Rosie wasn't really disappointed. She'd actually hoped he would change his mind. She wasn't looking forward to the long drive alone.

"We have to get supplies besides just the food stuffs you need, and I can help Gordon load. He'll appreciate it."

"Afraid I'll get on the first train out of town?" she teased.

"Nope. You love my children too much."

He was right, she did love the children. And she was beginning to care for their father as well.

She laughed. "I'll be glad for the company."

Wonderful! It would seem like a vacation. No more housework for one day. Oh, it would still be waiting when she got back, but that didn't matter. She was always behind anyway.

"Well, get moving," he said. "Daylight's burning. If you're real lucky I'll buy you noon dinner at Mary's."

Then he did the strangest thing. He playfully swatted her butt like they were an old married couple instead of newly wed and yet to bed.

"I'm on my way, just let me grab my bonnet and a jacket."

"Better grab a rain coat."

"I don't have a rain coat. The research

I did indicated that this is a dry climate."

"We are a dry climate, but that doesn't mean we don't get rain." He went to the coat closet and pulled out a rain slicker. "Here. Take this one. It was Sarah's and I just never seemed to get rid of it."

She took the slicker from him, glad of it and wanted to burn it at the same time. He'd done a pretty good job of removing all traces of his late wife, but every once in a while she found something. Bath salts in a drawer in the commode under the pitcher and basin; a blouse still hanging in the wardrobe mixed in with his shirts. Rosie had gotten rid of the things herself, not wanting any reminders of the woman who was still making life miserable for those she left behind.

She put the slicker underneath the buckboard bench and Tom helped her up onto it.

"You're still going to drive today," he said.

She nodded. "I'm ready for this, but a little nervous at the same time."

"I'll be here if something goes wrong. Just remember to keep their heads up and swat their butts to keep them going."

Rosie took a deep breath and flicked the reins onto the horses' butts. "Giddy up."

To her great relief, they started moving.

She looked over at Tom and a grin split his face. She'd like to see more of those.

He didn't make her drive the whole trip, thank goodness. She was so nervous, that by the time he took the reins, her back hurt so badly from holding tension while she drove the buckboard, she could hardly move. A groan escaped her as she relaxed against the back of the bench seat.

"You're going to have to learn to relax more when you drive or you won't be able to move when you get to town. You'll be coming to town on your own sometimes."

"I expected to at some point, but why do you say so?"

"Because when I'm with the cattle, whether during branding season or on a cattle drive, I won't be able to take you. You need to learn to do things by yourself."

"I'm surprised you'd let me go anywhere by myself. Aren't you afraid I'll leave and never come back?"

"I'm prepared for the day you leave. But I won't have you be a prisoner just to prevent it. I have to be able to trust you. So I do. Besides, you're not the type to go when you're wanted."

"So you finally believe I'm going to stay?"

"No. I still figure you'll leave, just not right away."

"You're just crazy. She has made you crazy. I'm not leaving. Not today, tomorrow, or anytime. You're stuck with me, Tom." She took off her riding gloves and slapped them to her lap. "You better get used to it."

He just smiled at her little tirade. "We'll see."

By the time they got to town, Rosie's anger had long since burned away. The rest of the trip was enjoyable. She and Tom talked about mundane things; talked more than they had in the previous month put together.

He pulled up in front of the mercantile.

"You go do what you need to do inside. I'm going to the bank and I've got other errands to run. I'll be back here in about an hour."

"Good. It will give me a chance to catch up on all the latest gossip from Sadie."

He walked away shaking his head and muttering, "Women."

She smiled and went inside.

"Hi, Mrs. Harris. How're you settling in?"

"First, call me Rosie, and second, I'm settling in rather well I think. Once I get my chores down pat, I'll be fine. The kids are wonderful and Tom, well he's Tom. What else can I say?"

Sadie nodded sagely. "Well, give me your order and we can talk while I fill it."

"Before we do the regular order, do you have a catalog of ladies clothing that I could look through? Maybe I'll have you order something for me."

"I've got all sorts of catalogs, from Sears & Roebuck to Montgomery Ward to Madam Trousseau's book of lingerie. Which one you want first?"

"That one," she pointed at Madam Trousseau's book, "I want to look at that one."

Sadie looked at her a little puzzled, but gave her the catalogue. It was a thin tome, probably forty or fifty pages.

Rosie started perusing it quickly. She had to have this done long before Tom got back.

"Can you order anything out of here?"

"Sure. What do you have in mind?"

Rosie pointed at the picture of a white negligee.

"Wow! That's one pretty piece of frew frew. You must have something special coming up."

"Oh, I do." It was all she was going to say. Telling Sadie anything was like telegraphing it all over town. She was taking a chance ordering this as it was. "Sadie, you have to promise me you won't say anything to anyone about this. Please. It's very important."

"Alright. You can count on me. But when it comes in, I expect you to let me in on the secret. Deal?"

"Deal." She hoped by that time she wouldn't have a secret, wouldn't need what she'd just ordered, wouldn't have to seduce her husband. She hoped he will already have seduced her.

*****

The next morning, after breakfast, Tom took Rosie aside.

"I have something to teach you."

"As much as I'd just *love* to learn something else I have to do, I have to clean upstairs and change all the linens today."

He shook his head. "That can wait. We'll sleep on the same sheets for another week. This is important."

"Alright. What is so important?"

Tom took a deep breath. "You need to learn how to shoot."

"No, I don't." She turned to leave.

He put a hand on her shoulder, halting her escape. "Yes, you do."

"Why?"

"Because when we drive the cattle to summer pasture and again to the railhead in Creede, you'll be here alone."

"Why don't you leave someone here to protect us, if you're that worried?"

"It's the children's safety I'm worried about, and I don't have any spare men."

"Really? Is that all? Just the children?"

"Of course. You have to be able to protect them at all times," he turned away and mumbled under his breath, "and yourself, too."

She heard him and smiled. By the time he turned back to her, she demurely held her hands together in front of her, no smile on her face.

"Who would teach me?"

"I will, of course."

"I didn't think you'd want to take that much time out of your day. After all, it might be difficult for me to learn."

He patted her on the back. "You can do it. You've learned everything else easily; this won't be a problem for you."

"Alright. If you insist."

"I do. It's important for a woman out here to protect herself. Take Catherine, for instance. She can use a gun almost as well as Duncan and has had to do it. There was some trouble years ago, before they were married. She had to protect herself from a very bad man. She was able to do it because she could use a gun and they knew it."

They walked out behind the barn. Tom carried a shot gun and had his pistol in its holster, strapped to his leg. Rosie figured he was going to teach her how to fire both weapons. She smiled.

"Alright," he said when they were at the targets. He'd set up several cans on the hillside for her to practice on. He took his pistol out of its holster. "This is a Colt .45. It can shoot six times without reloading." He handed it to her.

She nearly dropped the darn thing and had to grasp it with both hands. "It's much heavier than it looks."

"It is." He came to her side. "Now, pull the hammer back to cock it."

Rosie pulled the hammer back with her thumb.

"That's right. Now bring the gun back up and use the site at the end of the barrel to aim your bullet. Got it?"

She nodded.

"Now, gently squeeze the trigger."

It seemed to take forever. She squeezed and closed her eyes, opening them in time to see the dirt fly below the targets.

"Rosie, you have to keep your eyes open. Here let me help you." He came behind her and put his arms around her, holding her hands up. "Now squeeze again and keep your eyes open. You can't hit a target you can't see."

She took a deep breath and squeezed the trigger. The bullet hit to the right of the center can.

"Better. Let's try that again."

Tom moved closer to her. She felt his erection press into her back. He really wasn't immune to her. How long was he going to hold out? Did he really plan on never making love to her? Based on the current state of affairs, she didn't think he'd be able to hold out much longer. She wiggled her butt against him and corrected her stance. She heard his sharp intake of breath and smiled.

She fired again and again missed the target. This time to the left of the can.

"I'm getting closer."

"Yes, you are," he breathed into her ear. "Very close."

"Tom I…"

He stepped away and cleared his throat. "You've got the idea now. Try it again."

Rosie fired, and this time hit the can. A little low, it went flying into the air. Frustrated, she said, "Give me the shotgun."

"We haven't gotten there yet."

"And at this rate we never will. Just give me the shotgun."

He handed it to her. She grasped it, put it snug against her shoulder and fired at the cans. The one on the left went flying. She cocked it and fired again. This time the right one went flying into the air.

"I thought you couldn't shoot."

"I never said that. I've never shot a pistol, but I'm damn good with a shotgun. We used to shoot clay pigeons at Robert's club."

"Why didn't you tell me?"

"Why didn't you ask?"

He shook his head, turned and walked away, muttering, "Women."

Rosie chuckled to herself. That'll show him not to take her for granted.

*****

Every day rolled into the other, without much change. She was too tired to even think about seducing Tom; didn't have the strength to put any effort into it. She bathed in the evening before going to bed. After her bath, she braided her hair and crawled into bed, always before Tom. By the time he finally came to bed, she was sound asleep.

Tom saw the toll the work took on Rosie, but she never complained. He knew he needed to get her some help. There were several women in town, older ladies who had helped him out before, after Sarah left. And when his mother had to leave, they helped him again. He'd let them go when he knew for sure Rosie was coming. Now was the time to bring them back. Rosie deserved it. He didn't want her to be a slave, he wanted her to be able to mother his children, raise them better than he could, and she was doing that. Even with all the work she had to do, she still made time for them. It warmed his heart to see them together.

"I'm going to go to town today," he told Rosie one morning. "I'll be back before supper."

He watched the play of emotions on her beautiful face. Excitement, then disappointment at the realization she wasn't being asked to go.

He was such an ass.

But she'd thank him once he got back. He wasn't actually going to town, just over to the Walden ranch. John Walden's spinster sister lived with him, much to the chagrin of John's wife. The gossip all over the valley was that the wife and the sister didn't get along. He'd see if the sister, Agatha, would consider coming to live with him to help out Rosie. When he ran into her in town, she'd hinted that she'd like to come to work for him. That was when Rosie arrived more than a month ago.

Agatha was in her fifties if she was a day. A sturdy woman well used to ranch work. With her help, Rosie would have more time to spend with the children and that was why she was here, why he'd married her.

Who was he kidding? He'd married Rosie because he wanted to. The preacher was as surprised as anyone when he'd shown up with Rosie that first day. But as soon as he saw her, Tom knew he couldn't let her go. She was perfect, even as bedraggled as she'd been.

Her traveling suit showed off her hourglass figure. She'd put her glorious hair in a bun under her hat, but tendrils had escaped and formed a halo in the sunlight.

Even with the smudges of dirt on her face, she'd been beautiful. He'd planned on getting to know her a little more before marrying her, so his instant decision to wed had taken him by surprise as much as it had her.

He didn't want a woman, he'd told himself often enough he almost believed it.

But he wanted Rosie.

He wasn't stupid. He knew he was afraid to get close to anyone again. He put up walls so he wouldn't get hurt again. It was the natural thing to do after Sarah had taken all he had to give and thrown it back in his face, so why did he want Rosie? She was kind, gentle, caring, and pretty. She'd cared about his kids and their futures before she'd even met them. She might even love them. Something their mother hadn't. He couldn't risk letting her go. It wasn't fair to keep her at arm's length, he knew that. And she was determined not to stay there.

Every night when he got into bed she rolled over and cuddled against him. She did it in her sleep, and he was sure she didn't know. She was too tired to wake. It was just a natural instinct. One he liked very much. He'd wrap his arms around her and hold her softness to him, while she didn't know, couldn't see his weakness.

And smell. She always smelled so good. Just like roses. It was her cream, he knew, but it didn't matter. It was also Rosie. Tonight, he held one of her hands in his. It was red and rough despite the cream, the work having taken its toll on her beautiful soft skin. She would still have to do the cooking, gather eggs and milk the cows, but he could at least get someone in to do the laundry and clean the house.

Leaving the ranch after breakfast and his morning chores, he took the buggy and wondered if Rosie thought it odd, but if she did, she didn't mention it. He felt sure Agatha would come home with him, as he knew how intolerable she found her current situation.

Three hours later, he returned to the ranch, a small gray haired lady beside him. She was short, but stout and strong. He'd explained to her that he wanted her for laundry and general housework, and that he'd pay her ten dollars a month plus room and board, if she accepted. He had a spare bedroom off the kitchen for just such a purpose. Sarah had insisted that she have help. Help! He'd had several different women come to assist her.

One, Bertha, lived in while others came on a sporadic basis. Sarah did the cooking and taught Ben. She wasn't very good at either, but she did try. He'd have to give her that. Bertha did the laundry, which included changing all the linens and the ironing, and cleaned the house. Those poor women had done everything for Sarah. All Sarah had to do was cook and watch the children. Even that was too much in the end.

And Rosie had been doing it all. Everything. And doing a damned good job, if truth be told. All without a complaint.

Pulling up in front of the house, he brought the team to a stop and jumped down. He went and helped Agatha down, then got her bags and took them in the house.

"Rosie. Rosie," he called.

She came out of the kitchen wiping her hands on a kitchen towel. "Keep your socks on, I'm coming."

Finally she looked up and came to a stop. Then she came forward with her hand extended and a smile on her face. "I'm sorry. I should have been here to greet you. Tom, would you introduce me to your friend?"

He set Agatha's bags down. "Rosie, this is Agatha. She's here to help you with the housework. Agatha, this is my wife, Mrs. Harris."

Agatha grabbed Rosie's hand in both of hers and shook it. "Very pleased to meet you, Mrs. Harris. I think we'll get on fine. You just tell me what you want me to do."

Rosie looked up at him with tears in her beautiful brown eyes. Then she went to him and wrapped her arms around his neck and gave him a kiss. "Thank you. Thank you for seeing I needed help."

Tom couldn't help but put his arms around her. She leaned into him and he wanted nothing more than to kiss her until she begged him to stop and take her to bed. He gave her a small squeeze and set her away from him.

"You're welcome. I'll take Agatha's bags to her room and you can help her settle in."

Rosie nodded. "Please follow me. I'm so pleased to have you here."

"As I am to be here, Mrs. Harris."

"I hope you like it here, Miss Agatha. I'm afraid I've been a little overwhelmed. Poor Tom and the children have suffered for my lack of knowledge about doing all the things that need doing."

"Oh, I'm sure I will. Have you been doing for yourselves and the men, too?" asked Agatha, aghast.

"Well, yes, though I don't think I do it very well."

"Child, you should have had help before now. You've been trying to take care of fifteen people by yourself. It can't be done. You need help, and that's where I come in. You do the cookin' and teachin' the kids, I'll do the laundry and the ironin'. I can't cook worth beans or I'd help you with that as well. We can clean the house together. That should help you have a little time to relax at the end of the day, and not be too much for either of us to handle. Whatcha' say to that?"

"I say I think you're an angel."

Tom followed the women with Agatha's bags, listening to the conversation, and feeling ten times the heel. He should have gotten Rosie help to begin with. He knew it was too much for one person. It would have been different if it was just him and the kids, but with the eleven cow hands included, it was too much for one person. Any one person. Was he hoping to drive her away? Maybe he was. Trying to prove Rosie was no different than Sarah and would leave him. But she hadn't. She'd taken everything in stride and, other than that second night together, hadn't tried to get him to touch her. She was too tired.

Now that she had more time, and hopefully got more rest, would she go back to trying to seduce him? He had to admit, it was flattering to his ego, that she wanted him.

Sarah had never wanted to have sex and, once she was pregnant, they didn't. Ever. She said it wasn't good for the baby. But he had friends, like Duncan McKenzie, who said they had sex with their wives well into their ninth month. Duncan said Catherine wanted sex more than ever when she was pregnant. So it was just Sarah. Pregnancy was a good excuse for her not to allow sex.

What if he let Rosie seduce him? He wanted to touch her, feel her shiver and cry out with pleasure. He wanted to bury himself deep inside her, and watch her beautiful brown eyes as she came. Was it so wrong to want your wife? He'd just be sure not to fall in love with her, so when she left, it wouldn't hurt.

Yes, he could enjoy his wife while she was here. He was looking forward to what she'd try next. What if she'd quit trying? Maybe she didn't have any interest anymore. No, he was sure Rosie wanted children. She was an innocent; didn't know that he could prevent her getting pregnant by pulling out before he came. Then he could still enjoy his wife without worrying about more children to raise alone.

But a little voice in his mind told him Rosie wouldn't leave. She wasn't Sarah; wasn't remotely like Sarah. She'd already proved that.

CHAPTER 7

Tom was in his study when Rosie found him.

"Can we talk for a minute?"

"Of course. Sit down," he said, pointing at the chairs in front of his desk.

"I'll get right to the point. Since I have more time on my hands, I think we should go on a picnic. Just you and I. You could show me the ranch and then we could have a nice lunch. Perhaps in a pretty meadow or by a creek. You know your property and where a good spot for a picnic would be."

"That's a good idea. When did you want to go?"

"Now. I mean, how about today. I've already got the food ready to go."

He smiled. "Pretty sure of yourself, aren't you?"

"I am. You wouldn't deny me on such a beautiful day."

Tom shook his head. "You've got me pegged. Let's go. I'll get the horses and you get dressed for riding."

"Riding? I thought we'd take the buggy."

"Can't take the buggy where I want to go. We'll go slow. You can wear those pants that Catherine gave you. She said they'd come in handy."

She nodded. "She did say that, but I thought she was kidding. It's not decent for a woman to wear pants in Philadelphia."

"This isn't Philadelphia, and since we don't have a side saddle, you don't have much choice, if you want to go on this picnic. And I know a great place. There's even a nice little crick for wading, if you like."

"It does sound perfect. I'll get changed and put our lunch in saddlebags. Meet you out front in twenty minutes. Okay?"

"Deal. I promise I'll put you on a gentle horse. Don't worry about that."

"I wasn't worried…until you mentioned it." She turned on her heel, lifted her skirt and ran up the stairs.

She'd never worn pants before in her life, so was surprised at how comfortable they were. Tom had bought her a pair of boots, on one of their Saturday trips to town, which she'd also wear for the first time today.

She started unbuttoning her blouse at the top of the stairs. There would be no corset today. Not if she wanted to get in and out of her boots. She couldn't bend at the waist with the corset on, and she really did want to go wading. It had been so hot lately. The cold water on her feet would feel great.

When she reached their bedroom, she dropped her blouse on the bed and unlaced her corset. She put it in the bureau drawer and from the drawer below it, she pulled out her pants and put them on. They were a little snug, she was more filled out than Catherine was. Next she got out some socks that Tom bought for her and put them on, followed by the boots. She grabbed her blouse off the bed and put it back on over her chemise. It was strange and oddly freeing not to wear a corset. It was almost naughty to feel so good.

Excited didn't even cover how she felt. Ecstatic. Aroused. Thrilled. All these things at the same time. Butterflies whooshed around in her stomach. She gave herself the once over in the cheval mirror and liked what she saw. The pants accentuated her figure. Her legs were long, her waist small, and her breasts still round and firm. They wouldn't stay that way for long without the corset. Gravity had a way of bringing everything down in the end.

She hurried down the stairs to the kitchen. She'd hoped Tom would say yes, and made a picnic lunch for them. There were sandwiches of rare roast beef with butter, left over from supper the night before. A little cheese, some apples and four of her favorite sugar cookies.

In the pantry, she'd found a bottle of wine and a corkscrew. She gathered it all together, put it in the saddlebags, then put them on the front porch before going back in for a blanket to take along.

When she got back, Tom was waiting with two horses. He'd already put the saddlebags behind his saddle. She gave him the colorful blanket. It was a quilt that she assumed his mother had made. Based on what little Tom had said about Sarah, she doubted the woman had ever had the patience to do a quilt. Even with one of those new sewing machines, she wouldn't have done it. It was too domestic for her.

It was time to mount. She'd knew how to mount a horse. It was, after all, the best mode of transportation out here. But she'd never ridden astride. It would take some getting used to. Ladies in Philadelphia used a carriage or buggy, or rode sidesaddle. Come to think of it, riding sidesaddle was much harder than riding astride, so she shouldn't have any problems learning this in no time.

She took a deep breath and went to the left side of the horse.

"It's not that bad," said Tom. "I'll help you. Grab the saddle horn and put your foot in the stirrup and pull yourself up."

She did as he asked, putting her left foot in the stirrup and tried to pull herself up. It was harder than it looked. Then she felt strong hands on her waist lift her up. Oh my! Butterflies fluttered in her stomach and her skin tingled even as his hands left her. It was always the same. She craved his touch. And touch she would have this day. Rosie was determined to seduce her husband. Today.

They rode through the pasture toward the mountains, glorious in their majesty. It always took her breath away when she looked at the mountains. There was nothing like them. When she'd been on the train from St. Louis to Denver and first saw them rising out of the nothingness of the plains, she literally had lost her breath for a moment. She'd never seen anything so magnificent. And here, living among them, the feeling of being in the middle of grandeur never left her.

The path they followed was a rough track up the hillside. Pine trees lined the sides with chokecherry and sergeant berry bushes interspersed between the trees. When they reached the top, they looked down over a gorgeous green valley with a small lake on one end and a lovely little creek running south the length of the valley and out the other end into the mountains beyond.

"It's beautiful."

"I thought you might like it. This is one of our summer pastures. We'll be bringing the cattle up here for the summer and take them down to the railhead for shipping to Kansas City in September.

"Come on. I've got the perfect place for our picnic." He rode forward slowly, walking his horse, not only in deference to her lack of riding skills, but because the path was a bit steep.

Riding into the meadow at the bottom

of the hill, Tom nudged his horse into a canter, a much easier gait for the rider than a trot. Rosie's horse followed suit and though she was a little scared, she held onto the saddle horn and remembered to move with the horse.

Laughing, she pulled alongside Tom then overtook him, her horse in a full gallop. She rode to the creek.

"Whoa," she pulled back on the reins and stopped, waiting for Tom to catch up. "That was exhilarating."

Tom dismounted in one graceful move and came to her side. He reached up for her. She leaned down, put her hands on his shoulders and fell into his arms. He let her slowly slide down his body to the ground.

He was so strong, holding her like she was no heavier than Suzie. His member was hard and she knew he wanted her.

Her eyes locked with his and he held her close. Firm lips claimed hers as he crushed her body to him.

Suddenly he broke away and rested his forehead against hers. "Rosie, I want you." His chest rose and fell with each breath.

"I want you, too."

"But I don't want you here, in the woods like some floozy. Your first time should not be on a blanket in the dirt."

"I don't care."

"Well, I do. I want it to be special, something you'll remember always. Now, grab that blanket and I'll get the saddlebags before I change my mind. We'll leave the horses here and walk a ways downstream. It's not far."

They walked about one hundred yards downstream to an opening in the trees. Flat and grass covered, it was right next to the stream. The water looked inviting and about a foot deep. Rosie couldn't wait.

"Oh, how wonderful. And that stream is so clear I can see the rocks at the bottom."

She shook out the blanket, spread it

on the ground, then took the food from the saddlebags.

"Will you open this for me, please?" She handed him the bottle of wine.

"Where in the world did you get a bottle of wine?"

"It was in the pantry. Were you saving it for something?"

"No. I didn't know it was there. Sarah must have put it there. I knew she was drinking my whiskey, I didn't know she'd started buying wine. I didn't keep a close watch on the household accounts then. She was my wife. I trusted her."

The reference stung, but Rosie wasn't going to let anything mar this day. "Why don't you open the wine. We can let it breathe while we wade for a little while."

"Good idea." He uncorked the wine and set it between two good sized rocks so it wouldn't fall over and spill.

Rosie sat on a large boulder at the bank of the creek and took off her boots. She rolled her pants legs to about mid-calf, she didn't plan on going out too far. When she was done, she walked to the stream and waded in.

"Oh. Good Lord, it's freezing." She turned quickly to get out of the water. "Eeee! Tom!" On her backside in the freezing water, she hollered, "help me."

She tried to get up on her own and fell back into the water, drenching herself from head to toe. Tom ran to her and pulled her up into his arms, wading back out of the water.

"We've got to get you out of those wet clothes. I'll start a fire. It'll help them and you dry out." He set her down on the blanket. "Strip while I get some wood."

"What am I supposed to put on instead? I didn't bring any extra clothes."

"Wrap yourself in the blanket until your underwear dries, they'll be faster than the rest of your clothes."

Rosie peeled her wet pants off first, followed by her blouse. Tom was supposed to gather wood but couldn't take his eyes off of her. Her nipples were hard little peaks from the cold water and slight breeze. What may have felt wonderful to her five minutes ago, was now giving her shivers. Looking at her nipples, his body ached. Releasing a breath he didn't know he held, he turned away and picked up a piece of wood. Without looking back, he found another twig, then another and another until his arms were full.

When he returned to Rosie she had the blanket wrapped around under her arms and was sitting on a fallen log beside the ring of rocks used for a fire pit. She couldn't have been more beautiful wearing the fanciest ball gown. She'd taken down her wet hair and was combing her fingers through it, shaking it a little to make it dry faster. His fingers itched to be running through her beautiful hair. He was afraid if he got that close, he wouldn't stop with just her hair.

"How long do you think it will take to dry my clothes?"

"Too long," he muttered.

"What?"

"Not long. Once I get the fire going, I'll lay them on the bushes around here and put your under clothes on the rocks closest to the fire."

"I'm sorry. I had this all worked out and this isn't what I'd planned at all."

"Don't worry about it. Everything will work out all right. How about we go ahead with this picnic? Looks like you made some nice food for us. Want a sandwich?"

She pouted for a moment, "Yes, please."

He smiled. She was adorable, even pouting. He handed her a sandwich. "What are we supposed to drink the wine out of?"

"I packed two cups. They should still be in the saddlebags."

He rummaged around in the bottom of the bags until he found the cups. "Looks like you brought us cookies, too," he said bringing them up and out.

"I always have to have a cookie after

dinner. Didn't you know that?"

He shook his head. "No, there are lots of things I don't know about you. Why don't you tell me something about yourself and then I'll share something about me?"

"Alright. My birthday is September 23rd and I'll be twenty-seven."

"My birthday is May 30th and I was thirty-five."

"You don't look a day over thirty-four."

His bark of laughter made her smile. "You have a good sense of humor."

"I try. Working for you I need one."

That sobered him. "I'm sorry I've been such an ass. I never should have treated you that way, I have no excuse."

Rosie smiled at him and his spirits rose. "We got off on the wrong foot. You were hurt and betrayed by a woman you loved—"

"No, I never loved her."

She looked up at him with those beautiful brandy colored eyes of hers. "You didn't?"

"No. I know that now. I was angry that she left, but I was never hurt that she didn't love me. I didn't care about that. The kids, Ben, loved her. And he still misses her. I'm angrier about that than anything. How could she hurt the kids like that? How could any mother?"

"I don't know, but they're lucky. You're a good father."

"Thanks. They are my world. I don't know what I'd do without them."

"I don't either. Now that I know them, I love them so much. You must know that. I think they are amazing, and you're the reason for that."

"I think you're amazing." He moved closer on the log to her.

She looked down to where her feet were hidden under the blanket and blushed. He knew she blushed all over. Her neck and chest were as red as her face under his praise.

He raised her chin with his finger. "Look at me, Rosie."

She raised her eyes to lock with his. "Tom…"

He kissed her. Claimed her lips with a passion he was not sure of. She brought feelings from him he'd never felt before.

She wrapped her arms around his neck. Her blanket fell to her waist, baring her amazing breasts to him. He couldn't resist any longer. He broke away from her lips and took one of her turgid peaks into his mouth and sucked. Rosie's head fell back and she braced herself with locked arms on the log. The stance brought her nipple more firmly into his mouth.

He smiled at his responsive little bride. When he finally made love to her, she was going to amaze him. He already knew it. She responded more than any woman he'd been with before. She liked what he did to her. There was no way to disguise her responses.

He let go of her nipple and moved his lips back to hers. Kissing her completely. "I think your underclothes are dry now."

"Hmm?"

"Your chemise and bloomers. I think they are dry now."

Her eyes flew open. "Oh. Yes, of course." She reddened and turned away.

"Rosie."

She looked up at him.

"I mean to finish this soon."

She swallowed and nodded.

"Real soon."

*****

Agatha may have taken over the laundry, but Rosie still had a lot to keep her busy. The fatigue finally caught up to her. She took her normal nightly bath. She'd gotten some bath salts at the mercantile and got in the tub to have a relaxing soak. She awoke to strong arms lifting her from the cold water. She wrapped her arms around his neck and held on tight hoping, she could hide herself.

"Rosie? Are you all right?"

"I'm just tired. The bath salts relaxed me too much. You can put me down now."

He set her down long enough for her to wrap herself in a towel, then he swooped her up into his arms again.

"Tom!"

Walking to their bedroom, he said, "I should have seen how tired you were. Maybe I did and I ignored it. Either way, it's my fault you're exhausted."

She wrapped her arms around his neck again and settled into his arms. "No it's not. I just haven't gotten everything into a schedule yet. I'll get it situated soon."

"Agatha will help you now. I'm sorry, Rosie. I should have hired someone before now."

He kicked the door to their bedroom shut behind him, took her to the bed and let her stand up. He took the towel, dried her off and, after he turned the covers down, told her to lie face down on the bed.

"Let me take care of you," whispered Tom.

He gently dried her. Then he took her rose cream and massaged her legs and feet. Long strokes, up the back of her legs with his hand and small circles with his thumbs working the muscles as he came down her leg, then back up, and the rhythm started again.

Her skin was soft under his touch even before he put the cream on. How someone could work as hard as she did and still have such soft skin was beyond him. But he liked it. He liked touching her. Wanted to touch her all over. This would do for now. This night was for her. To give back some of what he'd taken.

Holding her calf on his hip, he massaged the cream into the bottoms of each foot and each toe individually. Worked it in with his fingers. She moaned her pleasure. He wanted to hear that moan for another kind of pleasure he would give her. But not tonight. As much as his body ached for her, he'd resist…tonight. When he gotten her sufficiently relaxed and limp on that leg, he started the process all over again on the other leg.

Next he did her left arm. Rubbed all the kinks out of it and worked individual fingers 'til they were limp. Next was her back and shoulders. For this he took lots of the cream and kneaded her back muscles. Then he worked circles, then up and down using the strength of his upper body to get deep in the tired, tight muscles. Up. Down. Around. Over. And then he began it all again. He used his fingers on her shoulders, squeezing, and rubbing circles with his thumbs.

He applied all these same techniques to her buttocks. Her magnificent round buttocks. He wanted to take his fingers and explore her, taste her, but he kept telling himself now wasn't the time. This time was for Rosie. To give back to her and make her feel good. Up, down, up, down, around, loosening all the tight, sore muscles. He was amazed at how tight and sore her butt seemed to be. She moaned every time he pressed hard.

"Am I hurting you?" he asked as he stopped the pressure. Her breathing came in short pants and he thought she might be as turned on as he was.

"Yes, but don't stop. I didn't realize how sore I am there. This will help loosen me up and then I'll feel better."

"Okay, but it's time to do the other side. Turn over, please."

She turned over, face up. He had to close his eyes and take deep breaths to keep from taking one of her nipples into his mouth, they were so perfect. Pink and hard. He watched her beautiful brown eyes dilate. She felt it, too.

He sat on the bed next to her, took her arm in his hand and applied all the same magic that he'd done on the other one. Rubbed her until she was weak all over.

The last place he worked on was her face. He put the cream on only his fingertips and starting at her forehead he rubbed small circles with thumbs, smoothed the cream down her cheeks and neck.

He wanted to continue to look his fill at her beautiful body. It would be so easy to take her now. She was pliable, relaxed, instead, he covered her with the sheet and blankets.

He sat on the side of the bed and gathered her long hair into his big, calloused hand and began combing the tangles from it. It was so soft and fine.

"Tom, you've done so much. I can do my hair. It's such a mess."

She started to rise. He gently placed his palm against her chest.

"Let me do this for you. Don't think, Rosie. Only feel. Enjoy."

His soft, gravelly voice washed over her, eased her. Settled her. Soothed her.

He continued to weave his spell around her. Relaxing her. Giving back to her some of the care she so willingly gave to all of them.

He picked up her hair section by

section. When he'd done as much as he could do from the front, he had her turn to her stomach. He worked all the knots out of the shiny, gold mass. It reached down past her waist and was one of the more glorious things about her, though he thought she was the embodiment of the ideal woman. Rosie was the loveliest woman he'd ever seen. And now he'd seen all of her. From the flawless globes of her breasts, to her small waist and generous hips, she was perfection.

After he combed the tangles from it he decided to brush it 'til it was dry. Taking a section at a time, he brushed until it shone. Liquid gold. It seemed a shame to braid it when he'd taken so much time with it, but knew if he didn't, it would be a mass of tangles in the morning.

"I'd love to have your glorious curls around us as we make love," he whispered softly. But she was asleep. Knowing she couldn't hear him, he said all the things he'd like to do to her. "I want to feel you around me. I want to make you come in every way I can think of. I'm going to tongue you, watch that pretty little bud of yours stand up for me to lick until you shatter."

Watching her, he undressed. She was so beautiful even in her sleep.

He crawled in bed next to her and wrapped her in his arms. Then he kissed her forehead, down the side of her face, her temple, her jaw. Whisper soft kisses. Touching her, brushing her skin and moving down. He moved down the side of her neck, feathering the kisses down, then back up to her lips. Teasing her with little butterfly kisses on the corners of her lips. Then he stopped and looked at her.

His kisses woke her and he watched her eyes open.

"This is something I've wanted to do since the day I picked you up on the train platform."

He took her lips with his. Gently he rubbed his tongue along the seam of her lips and she opened for him. But he didn't rush in, rather teased her tongue, entering little by little, dueling with her at each little move, until he had her completely. Then he feasted on her. His tongue in and out, around her mouth, then setting the rhythm he'd like to be doing someplace a bit lower with another part of his anatomy. But not yet. Tonight was just for Rosie.

He heard her excited, short breaths. Moving lower, he took one turgid nipple in his mouth. She gasped as he sucked it inside his greedy mouth while he rolled the other with his fingers. He sucked it and raised his head 'til it left his mouth with a "pop". Her hands were in his hair, kneading his head while he moved lower. Tonight he would give his Rosie an orgasm, probably her first.

He kissed his way to her nether lips, then parted her thighs to lie between them. Now his head was perfectly placed to love her with his mouth. He slid his tongue up her slit and poked it in to find her love bud hard and waiting for his attention. Which he was more than glad to give. Circling around the bud, he teased her. She lifted her hips to get closer to his mouth. He took the hint and suckled her clit while he entered her with one then two fingers. She was so tight, clamping around his fingers so hard he thought he was going to come just at the thought of what she would do to his cock.

Rosie grasped his head and bucked as

she shattered. She called his name and that of God in the same breath. When she finally settled, he kissed his way up her body again to her lips. Then he gathered her in his arms and laid back on the pillow.

"Sleep now, Rosie, love," he said.

She didn't hear him. Her eyes were closed and her breathing even.

She'd worked herself to the point of exhaustion. He'd let her. Watched it happen without seeing it until it was almost too late. She'd given her all to him and the children and never uttered one angry word about it. He'd worked her like a slave.

Now he'd try to make it up to her.

*****

Agatha was here and could handle things for a couple of days. Tom was going to take Rosie to town. They'd spend two nights at Mary's. He'd fill her with good food, then make love to her all day. Maybe he didn't deserve it, but he hoped she'd forgive him.

He'd take her shopping at Sadie's, for things for herself, not for the kids. Maybe take her on another picnic up in the hills above town. Far enough away from civilization that they could make love out in the open. He'd look his fill at her beautiful, perfect body, then he'd cover her with his and love her all the ways he knew how.

Do for her all the things he should have done when she first came. She deserved so much more than he had given her.

CHAPTER 8

Carolyn Vandenberg stepped off the train platform at Creede. As expected, no one waited for her. She made her way directly to the little house two blocks off Main Street and let herself in. Her brother never kept it locked. She guessed he didn't have anything worth stealing.

She'd lived in this backwards town for nine years. Nine years she'll never get back. But no one would recognize her now. Her new red hair color hidden beneath the plain bonnet she wore and new figure ensured that. She'd always been a skinny little thing with mousy brown hair, but no more. Now she had generous curves in all the right places. That's what happens when you aren't working your fingers to the bone every day. She wore cosmetics, too. Carefully applied powder, cheek and lip rouge, and coal black around her eyes made her unrecognizable as the clean faced woman who'd left.

Now she'd wait for her brother to get home and explain his letter to her. But in the meantime, she'd have a drink or two. She found his whiskey in the kitchen cupboard. Pouring herself two fingers of the amber liquid, she swirled it in the glass. So pretty. Even the worst rot gut whiskey had the same beautiful amber color as the smoothest single malt. She preferred the single malt, but would settle for the rot gut her brother drank. Any port in a storm, as they said in San Francisco. Or in her case, any drink was better than no drink at all. She took the bottle and filled her flask. She'd emptied it ages ago on the train.

If little brother would get home from his job at the bank, they'd make their plans.

*****

She'd had the best dream. Tom had massaged her all over with her rose cream until her muscles were totally relaxed and limp. He'd brushed her hair before climbing in bed and telling her all the most luscious things he wanted to do to her body. Ahhh. Only this time he made love to her. She felt all warm and cozy, inside and out. She didn't want to get up, even though the sun hit her in the eyes. The sun!!!

"Tom!" She turned over to find his side of the bed cold. He'd been gone for a while. Why didn't he get her up? He always got her up with a swat on the butt. This morning he was gone.

She threw off the covers and realized she was naked. Where was her nightgown? Her dream, was it real? How much of it was real? She didn't feel sore between her legs and there was no blood on the sheets. Wasn't there supposed to be blood on the sheets after her first time?

Raising her wrist to her nose, she sniffed. Roses. So it was true. At least part of it. Tom really had taken care of her last night. She'd been so tired. Even with Agatha here, she was still always tired. She put her hands to her cheeks, her face burning at the memory.

She grabbed her chemise, shoved her arms through the sleeves and yanked it into place. She followed that with her stockings, garters, shoes, corset, skirt, and shirtwaist blouse. Reaching for her hair, she realized Tom had braided it for her. How many men knew how to braid hair? She laughed. Her man did. Probably any man who was the father of a little girl. She unbraided her hair, brushed it 'til it shone and then twisted, forming it into a bun atop her head.

Checking the clock on the bureau she was amazed. It was already seven thirty. She'd slept right though breakfast and all of her morning chores. What about the men? Who cooked for them? They had to eat. Had Tom gotten Agatha to cook? Oh, those poor men.

She rushed downstairs to the kitchen. Tom sat at the table with a cup of coffee.

"There you are, Mrs. Harris. I was beginning to wonder when you were going to wake up."

"Why didn't you wake me?" She

poured a cup of coffee from the big pot on the stove. It always had coffee in it. The long standing policy of the kitchen was that the person who took the last cup had to make the new.

"You needed the rest. You've been working too hard, Rosie. It's time you had a break."

"What about the men? Breakfast?"

"Agatha fixed breakfast, yours is on a plate on the warming shelf. I did your morning chores along with mine. What I want from you is for you to eat breakfast, you're going to need your strength," he waggled his eyebrows at her. Was he teasing her?

"Then," he continued, "I want you to pack a bag for the two of us for a couple of nights away from here. We're going to town."

"Town? Why? Now that you have Agatha, you don't need me anymore?"

He got up and came over to her. Running a finger down her jaw, he told her,

"I'll always need you, Rosie. You can't get rid of me that fast. And I said pack for the two of us. Remember?"

"Then why town?"

"You need a break. You're working yourself to death, and I've been letting you. Well, I'm not going to let you anymore."

Rosie eyed him suspiciously. "What's gotten into you? First you rub cream all over my body, which I loved by the way. Then you brush and braid my hair. And you brought in Agatha and took me on a picnic, now this. Why are you being nice to me?"

Her words cut him like a knife. Had he really been that bad? He'd basically ignored her, except when she was sleeping. Then he allowed himself to touch her arm and run his fingers through the long end of her braid to the softest hair he'd ever felt

"I always should have been nice to you. You're not like Sarah, never have been, never will be. I'm sorry I treated you that way."

She stood, leaning against the counter.

155

"What are you saying? Exactly? I don't want to get it wrong. Are we going to have a real marriage? One where we actually talk to each other and get to know each other? Don't say yes and get my hopes up if you don't mean it."

Tears filled her eyes. He took her in his arms. "I don't blame you for not believing me. I want a real marriage, too. I won't rush you. There are still many things you don't know about me, and I about you. We should really get acquainted, don't you think?"

"I think I'm going to cry."

"Oh, Rosie," he chuckled. "This was supposed to make you happy."

"I am happy, you big lout." She buried her face in his shirt covered chest and bawled. Then she gave him little baby kisses all over his face while she cried some more.

Tom let her cry, knowing it was a step in the right direction. She had to get it out before she could move forward. He wasn't sure what changed for him. Her innate kindness, her determination, the love she gave to everyone, including him, changed him. He couldn't remain the harsh ass he'd been. She made him want to be good to her, to treat her like she treated them all.

He'd always liked Rosie, especially liked looking at her. Seeing her with the children, teaching them, not just how to read and write and cipher, but how to be good people. Even Suzie was learning to behave like a little lady, wasn't throwing her tantrums nearly as often and never in front of Rosie, because they didn't work. Rosie ignored her. In the beginning, that just made Suzie madder, but now, she was realizing she usually got her way if she asked nicely. And if it was something Rosie wouldn't let her do, she always sat Suzie down and explained it to her.

It was the way the men looked at her. With admiration. She treated everyone of them like family. She started baking special cakes and making their favorite meals on their birthdays. These were men who never celebrated anything, much less their birthdays, and here was Rosie, giving them each something special to look forward to.

It was everything about her. It was just Rosie. She didn't pretend she was something she wasn't. With Rosie what you saw was what you got. She admitted when she didn't know something, and was eager to learn. And Tom had discovered he was eager to teach her.

Tonight they'd have their wedding night. He'd ask Mary for a cold supper in their room. Mary usually had the bridal suite available and he'd get it. The cost didn't matter. It was the only room with a bathroom and the tub was big enough for two! He knew it because he'd helped get it there. They'd had to take off the outside wall and lift it with pulleys to get it in, and then rebuild the wall afterwards.

He intended on taking advantage of that tub to get Rosie all warm and pliable. Relaxed and wanting when he took her. He knew she was a virgin. The way she'd exploded in his arms proved that to him. She was untried and he was sure that had been her first orgasm. The first of many. Rosie wasn't going to know what hit her. The things he wanted to do to her and with her. He wanted to make love every way he could think of. By the time he was done, Rosie was going to be one satisfied woman, and wouldn't even think of leaving him.

She didn't plan on it now. He knew that. But it was there in the back of his mind, he needed to mark her. Make her his for everyone to see. What kind of caveman mentality was that?

He needed her. Wanted her. By the time this night was over, there would be no doubt of either in her mind.

*****

Carolyn sat on the sofa sipping the last of her brother's whiskey, trying to make it last, when he finally walked through the door.

"Where've you been? I've been waiting forever," she said.

"I can see how long you've been waiting." He picked up the empty whiskey bottle. "I've been working. One of us needs to have a real job now and again, so I can buy the good whiskey you like."

"This stuff was your best? Gracious, what would the rot gut taste like? Firewater, as the Indians call it?"

"We don't get single malt whiskey here in Creede. You got spoiled in San Francisco. Where's Frank?"

"Frank's not coming. I left him. He ran out of money. Don't look at me like that," she said when his lips turned down at the corners. "It's not like I was in love with him. And don't say I'm spoiled. I'm just getting what I deserve after all those years of drudgery I put up with."

"You came here hoping to snag yourself a rich miner and instead fell in love with a rancher. Oh, poor you."

She pouted. "That didn't last long. Before the first brat came, I knew I wasn't cut out for that life. I deserve the best. As you said, the best isn't available in Creede." Even the name of the town left a bad taste in her mouth. "The sooner I get away from here, the better. Now, how do we get a hold of that money?"

"I've done some thinking about that.

Two years I've been in this flea bitten town, waiting for this opportunity. Now it's come and you're going to help me. You're going to have to get one of those brats, as you like to call them. The boy's more likely to be alone. The girl is still too young to be going about on her own. But the boy... I've been watching. He goes out fishing and exploring by himself. Usually he has a book and finds a quiet spot to read. His favorite spot seems to be the barn. He goes there a lot, from what I've observed."

"Books! I'll never understand what people see in them. Give me the theater any day." She tossed her hair back over her shoulder.

"You do know most theater plays come from books originally, right?"

"Really? Who cares where they get it as long as it's up on the stage. I should have been an actress." She shoved a stray tendril of her bright red hair behind her ear.

"What do you mean, should have?"

Even in her half drunken state the sarcasm was not lost on her. She laughed.

He went to the small desk across the room from the sofa where she sat and unlocked the bottom drawer.

"Oh, you do love me," she exclaimed when he pulled the unopened bottle of whiskey out.

"Got nothing to do with that. I wanted to make sure there'd be some for me when I got home."

She frowned, rose unsteadily, and weaved her way across the room. "Pour me a drink, Sammy, and tell me how to kidnap my son."

*****

The trip to Creede from the ranch was only three hours without the detour to the McKenzie's. Tom had only those hours to make up for more than a month of the learning that he should have been doing. He'd found out more about her at the picnic, but not enough.

"So you wanted to get away from the evil sister-in-law? But there must have been easier, less drastic ways."

"Oh, there were for sure. But I wanted a home and a family of my own. You and Ben and Suzie are my family now. I'll do anything to keep all of you safe from harm. Those are my bonds to you. I adore the children, and I'm getting used to you." She grinned at him.

He chuckled. Rosie did have a good sense of humor. No wonder the men always smiled whenever she went by.

They went directly to Mary's when they got to town and found her in the kitchen. She did indeed have the bridal suite available. Not too many people wanted to pay the price for it, and certainly no one actually boarding with her would pay. It cost five dollars per night to rent. That was all some people made in a month. They sure weren't going to spend it on a room for one night. But for Tom, the price could have been double, and it still wouldn't have been too much. Not to make Rosie happy.

"Can we get a cold supper brought up to the room?"

"Ah. I understand. You don't intend on coming out this evening at all. You sly dog," smiled Mary. "You finally giving that sweet girl a honeymoon?"

He was sure he blushed, but Mary didn't seem to notice.

"Sure. I've got some leftover chicken and biscuits, a little cheese and some sliced apples that should do nicely. Would you like a bottle of champagne? I have a couple for special occasions. They're three dollars a bottle."

"You bet. Nothing's too good. I want to make this special for her."

"Why, Tom, is it possible that you've fallen in love with your wife?" Mary said with a wink.

He sobered for a moment. Had he? No, it wasn't possible. Not love. He just wanted to make things up to Rosie, that was all. "I want to make her happy. I've put her through a lot since we got married. I need to make it up to her."

"Take your bag up to the room and I'll see to everything else. Do you have something to do for a little while?"

"Yeah, Rosie wants to go to Sadie's and check on an order she made. Some books for the kids, I think. Then we'll be back here and I intend to keep her 'entertained' until morning. Tomorrow we might go on a picnic. What do you think? Can you fix us up with food?"

"Of course. It'll probably be the same thing you're having tonight. Chicken and biscuits do travel best."

Tom went out to the foyer where he'd left Rosie. She was looking at all the pictures Mary had hanging. There were some photographs, but mostly pen and ink drawings of what she assumed were areas around Creede. Mountains, meadows with flowers, a rolling river.

"Did Mary do these drawings?"

"I don't know."

"I'll have to ask her. They're beautiful. I haven't even gotten my drawing materials out of the drawer where I put them."

"You draw?"

"I dabble. You can't really call what I do art, but I enjoy it. I hadn't thought about it before, but maybe the kids would like to try it."

"Ben might. I don't know. Suzie will love it." Guilt washed over him. She hadn't had time to do any drawing or reading, or anything else she might have enjoyed. He'd been working her to the bone. No more, he vowed. Agatha was there and if he needed to hire another girl to help out, he would. "You wait here while I take the bag up to the room. I'll be right back."

When he came back down, Tom took Rosie's arm and they walked down to the mercantile.

"Mrs. Harris, there you are," said Sadie as soon as they entered. "Good to see you, too, Tom. I got in those books you ordered."

"Now Sadie, you know you're supposed to call me Rosie. Did you get that other item we discussed?"

Almost afraid to look, she glanced over at Tom, who cocked an eyebrow in question. She shook her head and felt the heat rise and knew she was living up to her name now.

"Sure did," said Sadie. "Come on back and see it."

"I'll be right back," she said as she followed Sadie to the back room of the store.

"Keep an eye on the front here, would you, Tom? Call me if you need anything," said Sadie.

"I'll be fine. You ladies go on."

The back room of Sadie's store was like a wonderland for women. This was where she kept her ready-mades. Dresses, chemises, nightgowns, corsets, blouses, and skirts. Everything the well-dressed rancher's wife might need.

She opened up a large cedar closet. "This is where I keep my 'special' items, like the one you're interested in. Don't get much call for something like this."

Sadie pulled the sheerest silk negligee

and robe out of the closet. The sheer confection was almost transparent. Rosie had never seen anything like it. It was beautiful white silk with lace edging. She held it up to herself and looked in the mirror.

"I don't know why someone as pretty as you would need something like this."

"To make him absolutely crazy, that's why." She grinned at Sadie. "Think this will work?"

"Absolutely," laughed Sadie.

This would do it. There was no way Tom could resist her. Just in case he changed his mind.

"Wrap it up. I'll take it."

Sadie smiled. "I can tell having you living here is going to make my life much more interesting."

"Now, don't be expecting this kind of order very often. Maybe once a year. By the way, do you know anyone who sews for hire around here? I need to get some clothes made for the kids and Tom, and start getting holiday presents going. I don't sew except maybe to replace a stray button now and again. Even then it's an iffy proposition"

"But, Rosie, it's only June. You want to start getting Christmas presents now?"

"Of course. You can never start your Christmas shopping too early. Especially with having to get most of it shipped in or made. That's another reason I want to find a seamstress. Suzie and Ben are growing out of just about everything."

"We've got some ready-made clothes for children that might get you through until you find your seamstress. I think I heard that Maggie Kelly is taking in sewing. Her husband's a miner. They live up by the mine at Bachelor."

"Bachelor? That's an odd name for a town."

"Not a town, really. Just a settlement. Lots of miners, a couple of saloons and that's about it. No store or church yet. They do have a whorehouse, though," Sadie said with distain.

"Oh, those poor women. Forced to make a living that way. How awful for them," said Rosie.

"I never thought of it that way. I always assumed they chose the life."

"I suppose some do, but I think that hardships of one kind or another lead those women to those straits. There but for the grace of God go I."

"Amen."

They walked back out to the front of the store. Tom was talking to Sam Kent, the bank president. Rosie left her purchases with Sadie to go and talk to them.

"Hello, Mr. Kent. How are you this fine day?"

"Very good, Mrs. Harris, and you?"

"I'm doing very well, and do call me Rosie."

Sam smiled at her. "Only if you'll call me Sam. I have a little confession to make." He leaned in and whispered so only the three of them could hear. "I'm terrible with names. I didn't remember your name is Rosie. But I'll do better. I promise I'll know it the next time we meet."

"I'll hold you to it." She looked over at Tom. "Tomorrow, I want to go up to Bachelor, can you take me?"

"Of course. It's pretty up that way. I wanted to take you on a picnic tomorrow anyway."

"Are you two in town for a couple of days? Finally getting a little honeymoon?" asked Sam.

Rosie blushed.

Tom answered. "We are. As much of one as you can get in two days." He leaned in and whispered to Sam, "and nights."

Sam laughed. "I'm delighted for you. Have a great time while you're here. Well, I best be getting back to the bank. Just out for a little walk when I saw you walk in here and thought I'd say hello."

"Have a good day, Mr. Kent, I mean Sam."

"Oh, I will, …Rosie. You, too."

Sam walked out of the store, whistling.

*****

Sam Kent walked quickly past the bank and to the little house where he lived. He went inside, directly to his sister's bedroom.

"Get up," he shouted at her, opening the curtains. "We have our chance now. Get the hell out of bed, you stupid drunken bitch." His anger at her hung-over state almost got the better of him.

"What the hell? Why are you yelling?"

"Because we have the perfect opportunity to get that boy, maybe the girl, too and you're too wasted to take advantage of it."

She shook her head. "I'm not. Tell me." Putting her feet over the side of the bed she sat up and then went behind the screen and used the chamber pot. She scratched her backside, yawned and stretched as she came from behind the screen.

"Well?"

"Tom and his new bride are here, in town, for the next two nights. Tomorrow they're going up to Bachelor for a picnic. We, meaning you, can snatch the children while they are gone."

"And how, pray tell, am I going to do that?"

"Look, no one knows you're my sister. And you don't look like the mousy little woman that left here with Frank two years ago. But I bet you can become that mousy woman again if you just wash your face. Put your hair up tight under your hat and the color isn't so noticeable. Right now it's dirty from the train trip and looks browner anyway."

"So, you want me to just ride up and take the kids out from under the nose of the help at the ranch?"

"Yes. Ben will still recognize you. He's missed you, though for the life of me I don't know why. He'll be more than willing to go with you. Leave the girl. You're going to be on a horse. Only room for two. You do still remember how to ride, don't you?"

"Of course." She went behind the screen again and took off her night-rail. "Do you still have my trunk with my old clothes in it?"

"In the attic."

"Get it. I'm going to need my riding gear."

"You can't wear your old garb anymore. You've gotten fat. I'll get some of my clothes. If they're a little baggy, all the better."

He left to get her the clothes. She came out from behind the screen wearing her chemise and bloomers. No corset today, not if she's to hide her assets. Long past the modest stage of life, she sat on the bed and waited for Sam to return.

Ten minutes later, he was back. He'd brought her old boots, some wool pants, a chambray shirt, wool jacket and hat. She dressed and looked at herself in the mirror.

"Not bad," she said to her reflection.

Sam sat on the bed and watched her dress. It was perfect, she could pass for a boy in the outfit. No one would think twice about a youngster riding out of town.

"I'll saddle one of my horses for you. I don't ride it much, so the horse won't be recognized as belonging to me. Besides, you'll be long gone before anyone sees that horse."

She put on her hat, cinching it under her chin. "Alright, I'm ready. Let's go. Where do you want me to take the kid?"

"There's that old abandoned miner's shack north of the ranch. You remember. You can hide out there until I come for you. I've written a ransom note which you'll leave at the ranch in a place someone will find it, but you won't get seen leaving it."

Carolyn nodded.

"And Sarah. Don't screw this up."

"I won't. You just do your job and

you'll have twenty five hundred dollars to do with as you please. And don't call me Sarah. I'm Carolyn. Sarah's dead."

CHAPTER 9

Tom carried all of the purchases except the "special" one back to Mary's. Rosie wouldn't let him carry that one, and made Sadie wrap it in plain brown butcher paper in the back of the store so he wouldn't see.

When they got to the room, Tom opened the door to their suite and ushered her in. The room was lovely and very well appointed. It had a tall boy dresser, chest of drawers, small table set for two with a platter of food on it. A beautiful cheval mirror stood on one wall with a Chinese changing screen next to it in the corner. And, of course, a bed. A brass bed with ornate scrolled head and foot boards.

The bathroom was immense. Rosie guessed they'd converted a small bedroom to the bathroom. It had a huge, claw footed bathtub that looked like it could easily accommodate two people. She couldn't imagine how they'd gotten it through the door. Although its size did give her ideas.

Her body ached, but she wasn't sure why. All she knew was she wanted to make love to Tom badly. The little surprise she had for him should help her seduce him. He was more open to making love since he'd given her the massage. Her face heated at the memory and she took a deep breath to squelch the feelings that it brought with it.

When Tom went down to see Mary, Rosie hurried to freshen up. She took her hair down, ran her fingers through it, loosening the curls. Tom liked her hair down. She'd seen it in his eyes. Tonight she was going to have it spread out on her pillow while he made love to her. Just like in those romance novels one of the maids back home loved to read. If making love was anything like what he did after the massage, she was going to like it very much.

She had a vague idea of what to expect. Her mother died before she could give Rosie the 'wedding night' talk. And it wasn't something her brother ever would have considered talking to her about. Just the thought of it mortified her.

Now was the time for seduction and she wasn't sure what she was supposed to do. Twenty-six years old and as naïve as a girl just out of the schoolroom! Well, not anymore. She was going to make love with her husband tonight. Whatever it took. Tom would be back shortly so, she went behind the changing screen, removed her clothes and put on the negligee.

By the time Tom came back, she was nervous as hell. Sure she was making a big mistake, she almost took off the negligee and put back on her clothes, but she decided it was better than waiting in her chemise and bloomers, or her regular nightgown. Both of which she decided weren't sexy at all, since Tom had seen her in both and seemed decidedly unaffected.

There was a knock on the door. Rosie opened it but stood behind it so he couldn't see her and neither could anyone else who happened to be passing in the hall. She wasn't about to parade about in the silky attire she now wore for all the world to see.

Tom carried a bucket with a bottle and ice in one hand and two glasses in the other. He set them on the table and turned around to say something. At least she thought he was going to say something. His mouth was open, but nothing came out. Then he smiled and she knew everything would be all right.

"You look beautiful."

She ducked her head, thoroughly embarrassed. "Thank you."

He walked over to her and lifted her chin until she looked him in the eyes. "You are the most beautiful woman I've ever known."

Slipping his fingers beneath the lapels, he slid the robe down her arms and into a puddle on the floor. Then he took her in his arms and kissed her. His tongue ran along the seam of her lips and she opened for him. He explored her, tasted her, and she him. He tasted of apple, clean and crisp. She wrapped her arms around his neck and hung on for the ride.

Tom backed her up until she ran into the bed. Then he kept going, lowering them onto the bed. He broke the kiss only to start again on her neck and the sensitive area behind her ear. Tickling the outside of her ear, his tongue sent shivers through her body.

"Tom," she moaned his name.

He kissed his way down to her collar bone and the little hollow at the base of her neck. He rained kisses on her until he reached her breast, then he licked the nipple through the silk and blew on the damp cloth. Her nipple beaded to a hard point and he took it into his mouth and suckled her through the silk of her gown.

Rosie about came off the bed. The sensations shot like an arrow straight to her core. Grasping his head, she pulled him down to her. Closer, she needed more. But he would have none of it. He moved to the other nipple and did the same thing while he rolled the first one between his fingers and gave it a little pinch. Sensations so foreign to her, and yet recognized by her body, rocketed through her. Pleasure-tinged lightning bolts shot from her nipples to her woman's center.

Suddenly he pulled her to her feet. "As beautiful as you look in this, I want you naked and if you don't take it off now, I'll rip it off you."

The lovely gown fell to a pool on the floor and she stood before him fully exposed.

"Now you. I need you," she said. "Need to feel your skin next to mine."

She reached for the buttons on his shirt at the same time he went for the ones on his pants. Soon he was nude and she was back in his arms, giving him the same light butterfly kisses down his neck as he'd given her.

"Slow down, sweetheart. We have all night." He took her face in his hands and ran his thumbs along her jaw. "And all day and night tomorrow, if we want. Come with me."

He led the way to the bathroom and turned on the hot water in the tub, adjusting it until it was the perfect temperature.

"Now, where were we? Ah, yes, I remember." He kissed her, held her with only his lips while his hands did wonderful things to her body. He feathered his fingers down her arms, across her chest until he came to her breasts, where his hands stopped their travel and cupped her full curves.

"God, you're amazing."

Her head fell back and her heart drummed in her chest, she'd never felt anything so wonderful. Then his hands were gone and she was bereft, needed them back. Her head snapped up and she looked at him. He'd turned to adjust the water and put bath salts in. The water was about halfway up the side of the tub, and he turned it off.

"I want you to get into the tub first, I'm going to get in behind you."

Rosie wasn't sure what he had in mind, but she trusted him. Things were progressing so nicely, Tom was making love to her, slowly, and in a way she'd never imagined. What in the world could they do in a bathtub? She got in as he asked and sat near the middle of the tub so he could get behind her.

He stepped in, slid down and then pulled her back against him. His rock-hard length pressed against her back as she settled.

"Lean your head back against my shoulder."

She did.

"That's right. Now close your eyes, Rosie. Relax and just feel."

"Tom, I…"

"Shh. Feel me." He'd soaped up his hands and ran them up and down her arms. Up to her shoulders where he massaged her aching muscles. She already felt calmer than she had since she'd arrived on that train platform a little more than a month ago.

His hands left her a moment before he used the washcloth to rinse her. He wrapped his arms around her waist, easing his hands up over her stomach, up again to each breast, over and around, tweaking each nipple then soothing it. His hands glided easily over her slick, soapy body.

Rosie leaned back against his chest and sighed. "This feels wonderful."

"Good. I'm glad." He licked the side of her neck, bit it softly and then suckled, marking her lightly.

She arched her neck and rolled her head away, giving him easy access to this sensitive part of her body.

His wonderful, talented hands moved down, caressed her belly, and continued downward 'til he reached her nether lips. Gifted fingers opened her and ran up and down her slit, around her pleasure bud and back down again.

She moaned. Without warning, he plunged one finger into her slick passage, bending it just enough to hit a particularly sensitive spot.

Her body clamped down around his finger. It felt so good. He slid another and then another inside her and moved them, stretching her, preparing her and pleasuring her.

She pressed back into him, needing the anchor his body provided. He pressed her little love bud and teased it with his thumb while he moved in and out of her with his fingers.

Pressure built within her. Glorious feelings. She was on a precipice. Needed something to send her off. He rubbed her little bud harder and she cried out his name while her body shattered. A thousand lamps couldn't compare to the lightning that whipped through her.

Soothing her until she settled, he said, "Let's get out of here. The water's cold and I have so much more to show you and do to you before this night is done.

They rose from the tub. Tom wrapped a towel around her before he grabbed one for himself. He wrapped it around his waist, then proceeded to dry her. Every inch of her. He paid special attention to her nipples, the fabric of the towel rough against them until they were hard as rocks. Little shocks went straight to her core each time he touched them.

Rosie couldn't help her moans. "God, what are you doing to me?"

"I'm making love to you. Something I should have done as soon as you got here. I'm marking you as mine. For always. Mine."

"Yours. Always." She took his beloved face between her hands. "I'm yours with or without your mark. You're stuck with me."

"I want you now, Rosie." He held her close and his erection pressed into her belly. "Feel how much I want you." He ground himself against her.

She nodded. Now was not the time to be shy. "Yes. I need you to come into me. Please."

"Get on the bed."

She lay down and then moved up until her head hit the pillows.

He rose over her, erect and ready.

CYNTHIA WOOLF

"I've tried my best to prepare you for this first time, but there's still liable to be some pain, and for that I'm really sorry."

Slowly, with infinite care, he entered her. Slick and ready for him, she felt nothing except wonder. This was so right. "More." It was frustrating he was going so slow and she wanted it now. But Tom wouldn't be hurried.

He entered then pulled back, a little more then pulled back again.

"I'm sorry, baby," he reared back and then slammed home, pushing through her maidenhead. She stopped breathing. Tom stopped moving.

"What now? Is that it?" she asked.

"God no. I'm just trying to let your body adjust to me."

"I think it's adjusted. I want to move, I want you to move. It's exquisite, but I need more."

Tom rested his forehead against hers. "You constantly surprise me."

He started moving in her. Slowly at first, then he picked up the pace. In. Out. Faster. Harder.

Rosie was awkward to begin with. Her strokes were off, but she soon got the rhythm and moved up at each of his down strokes and back when he did. She was so close to that precipice she'd been over once tonight. So close. "Tom," she panted, asking for completion without knowing the words.

But he knew. He reached between them and rubbed her little bud. He barely had to touch it before she fragmented again, calling out his name and invoking the name of God as well.

Tom pressed in once, twice, and grabbed her, burying his face in the crook of her neck. He groaned out his hot release deep within her. She hoped they'd made a baby tonight, but regardless, she was sure she'd have a lot more chances in the coming years.

"That was amazing," she said, once her breathing returned to normal. "Do I have this to look forward to very often, or just special occasions?"

Laughter rumbled deep in his chest and worked its way out. "Oh, you have this to look forward to at least nightly, and that's only assuming I can keep my hands off you during the day."

He rolled to his side, taking her with him, tucking her head on his shoulder. She loved the feel of him, the weight of his body on hers after completion. It was so…right. And yet this, cuddling, feeling his hard body next to hers, her leg draped over his thigh, was almost as good. Almost.

"Are you hungry?" he asked.

She sat up and grinned at him. "Famished. I seemed to have worked up an appetite. Let me fix us a plate. We can eat it in bed and pretend we're on a picnic."

He let her up and swatted her bottom when she stood.

"Oh!"

"Get me fed, woman," he said, laughing.

*****

Carolyn stood on the bluff overlooking the ranch. The place she'd spent nine years of her life. Nine long, boring years. Thank God Frank had taken her away from all of that. It may not have worked out with Frank, he wasn't rich enough for long enough for her tastes, but she'd fix that herself. She might even go back to him for a little while. Of course, with the seed money she was going to get from this little job, she could lure a rich husband. All she had to do was appear rich until it was too late for them to know the truth. It wouldn't be the first time a woman had taken a rich man for a ride. Anyway, they got to fuck her, that was worth the cost as far as she was concerned.

She thought back to her marriage. It was too bad Tom hadn't been rich. He'd been the only man to take his time and make sure she had pleasure when they had sex. Oh well, that was then, this was now.

Now she waited. Watched and waited. Finally she saw the boy go to the barn by himself. No one followed him. It was her chance. She knew the layout of the ranch, knew where to stay to remain out of sight. She walked her horse around through the trees to the north side of the barn, next to the forest. She left the horse tied to one of the trees and walked to the barn.

Ben was in one of the empty stalls reading a book when Carolyn found him.

"Ben?"

He looked up. Carolyn took off her hat.

"Mama? Mama, is that you?" Ben got up and ran to his mother. "Where have you been? I've missed you, Mama." He locked his arms around her waist.

Carolyn wrapped her arms around the boy and kissed the top of his head. "I had to go away for a while, but I've come back for *you*, Ben. Come with me."

"What about Papa and Suzie? And Rosie? What about Rosie?"

"I came back for you, Ben. Just you. I couldn't stand being away from you, from my baby, for any longer. Come with me now."

He nodded.

She smiled.

CHAPTER 10

Tom and Rosie lay in bed. Both sweaty. Both satisfied.

There was a knock at the door.

"Just a minute," called Tom.

"Hurry, Tom, it's important." The urgency in Mary's voice made Tom jump out of bed and jam his legs in his pants. Rosie brought the covers up to her neck.

He went to the door and threw it wide.

"What's wrong?" he asked Mary.

"Charley from your ranch was just downstairs. He said to tell you Ben is missing, and to give you this." She handed him a plain envelope. Written on the outside: *For Tom Harris*. "They found it tacked on the barn door."

Tom ripped the envelope open. Inside was a lone sheet of paper.

If you want to see your boy alive again bring $5,000 and leave it outside the abandoned mine shack two hours north of your ranch. Leave it by the well on the side facing the door.

He rammed his fingers through his hair.

"Damn! God, damn!" he shouted.

Rosie threw back the covers. It was only Mary, after all, and now was not the time for modesty. She grabbed the negligee's robe from the floor and went behind the Chinese screen where the rest of her clothes were.

"Thanks, Mary," said Tom. "Would you send someone for the sheriff?"

"Already have. Soon as your man told

me that Ben was gone, I took the note and sent him on to get Dan."

Rosie came out from behind the changing screen fully dressed.

Mary left, shutting the door behind her.

"Who would do this? Tom, why would someone take Ben?"

"I don't know. I'm not a rich man. I do well enough, but I'm not rich. You know that."

Before she could answer, there was another knock at the door. Rosie answered it this time, while Tom finished dressing. There was a tall, blond man who looked like any other cowboy, except he was wearing a star on his chest. She guessed this was the sheriff.

"Dan, thanks for getting here so soon." Tom went over and shook his hand.

"I came immediately."

"Rosie, this is Dan Baker, the county sheriff."

"My pleasure, Mrs. Harris. I wish we were meeting under better circumstances."

"So do I, sheriff." She took his hand. It engulfed hers.

"What do we know?" asked Dan.

"Someone has kidnapped Ben and is holding him in exchange for five thousand dollars."

"Five thousand dollars is a hell of a lot of money."

"Why would someone do this? I don't have five thousand dollars." He slammed his fist into the hard wood of the wall.

She doubted he even felt the pain.

"No, but I do, or very nearly. Twenty-five dollars short of that. Remember?" said Rosie.

She said it calmly. No need in both of them being crazy. She'd leave that emotion for Tom right now.

He looked at her, "You don't think that I—"

"No! Don't even say it. Someone is out to hurt not only you, but me. I would never, ever believe that you would use my feelings for Ben against me. Let's look at this logically."

"How can you be so calm?" he demanded.

"It won't do any good for me to cry and carry on. That's exactly what I want to do, but it won't bring Ben back."

"You're right. I'm sorry." He hugged her to him. "I'm just worried."

"I know. So am I."

Dan interrupted, "Other than you two and me, who else knew about your money?"

Rosie had forgotten he was in the room.

"No one," said Tom.

"Not true," said Rosie. "Anyone working at the bank could have known. There could have been someone who overheard me telling you I need to deposit it, though I don't remember anyone being near.

We were lucky. It was just as it opened that we went to the bank and there were no other customers yet. For sure Sam Kent, but it could be anyone who works there."

"There are only two tellers in addition to Sam. It had to be one of those two."

"Three," said Rosie.

"What? Why three?" asked Tom.

"I'm not ruling out Sam Kent. Here," she handed him his socks out from under the bed.

Tom pulled them on, followed by his boots.

"You can't seriously believe Sam had anything to do with this. He's the bank president ,for Christ's sake."

"It's unlikely, that's true, but we can't rule anyone out," she insisted.

"Fine."

The two men sat at the table. Rosie stood behind Tom.

"There could be a lot of suspects, but the most likely are those at the bank. Sam, Joshua and Pete are the only people who work there. So it would have to be one of them," said Dan.

"Or someone they might have told," said Rosie.

"She's right," said Tom. "They all have family they could have told. Well, all except Sam. He doesn't have anyone that we know of."

"How long have you known Sam?" asked Rosie.

"Less than two years. Isn't that right, Dan?"

"Yeah, he came just after you got that telegram about Sarah," said Dan.

"And he's never had anyone come visit that I know of," said Tom.

"That still doesn't eliminate him," insisted Rosie. "After all, he's the only one we told directly. He's the one who did the deposit."

"But who would he tell?" countered Tom.

"I don't know. None of it really matters until after we get Ben back." She started pacing the room.

"Rosie. It's everything you have. I can't ask you for your money. I'll take a mortgage on the ranch."

"You most certainly will take the money. Everything I have and all I need is you, Ben and Suzie. You're all that matters."

Tom took her in his arms and kissed her. "I'll make it up to you. Someday I will," he whispered for her ears only.

"You already did." She smiled and ran her finger down his jaw to his chin. "You gave me a family of my own."

Dan cleared his throat. "Sorry to interrupt, but I have to agree with Mrs. Harris, er, Rosie. I'm not eliminating anyone just yet."

"You know best," said Tom. "The bank won't open 'til tomorrow. But I'm going to see if Sam will open it now. Hell. We don't even know if he has that much cash on hand.

"What if he doesn't? How will we get the money? If anything happens to Ben...." She stopped long enough to ask the questions and then paced the floor again.

Tom grabbed her by her shoulders. "It won't do any good to wear a hole in Mary's rug."

"What about Suzie? Is she all right? We need to get home now," worried Rosie.

"Suzie wasn't mentioned in the note or by Charley. Let's go talk to him first. Then I'm sending instructions back with him. Everyone is to be armed and Suzie doesn't leave the house for any reason. We'll go back once we get the money. Dan, will you ride with me when I take the ransom to the drop off?

"You bet. Until you leave it by the shack, me and that money are one."

"Thanks. I don't want to leave Rosie or Suzie alone. I can't take a chance with either of them. But once we get to the ranch, I'll have one of my men with them every minute I'm not."

Rosie stopped her pacing. It was the nicest thing he could have said, and she was sure he didn't realize its implications. He cared for her. As soon as they got Ben back, she was going to explore this, but right now Ben was the only one that mattered.

The three of them walked over to Sam Kent's house. They knocked, waited, and were about to leave when the door opened. Sam stood there with a towel around his neck and his undershirt on.

"Tom, Rosie, and Dan, too. Goodness gracious, to what do I owe the pleasure?"

"Sam, I need you to open the bank and give us Rosie's money," said Tom with no preamble.

Sam cocked his head to one side. "Tom, I can't do that. We open at nine tomorrow morning. You know that."

"It can't wait, Sam. Someone's kidnapped Ben and is demanding five thousand dollars to return him."

Sam closed his eyes and shook his head. "Tom, I'm so sorry. Of course, I'll open the bank. Let me grab my shirt." When he got back he said, "You got lucky. Normally there is no way I'd have that much cash on hand, but the mine payroll arrived yesterday, so there's plenty to cover this." He paused for a moment. "Do you think whoever did this knew the cash would be here now?"

"I don't know," said Dan, "but I don't believe in coincidences."

CHAPTER 11

She had to wait at the mining shack until they dropped off the money. Then she'd leave the boy there where he could be found, and hightail it out of this podunk backwater town forever.

Carolyn tied her horse far back into the trees, hobbled it with plenty to eat so it should stay happy and quiet. Unfortunately, she'd had to tie up her son and gag him. He wouldn't stop crying about leaving his sister and father. Now he just sat in a corner and stared at her. She wished he'd look away. The condemnation in his eyes was almost enough to make her regret what she was doing. Almost.

She watched through a hole in the wall. They were supposed to leave the money and ride away. The front of the shack faced a large meadow and she'd be able to watch them go and see if they stopped or veered off the path.

Finally, she saw two horses. Her heart raced and her stomach roiled. Now was not the time to be sick. Tom and Sheriff Dan. Good, that's how it was supposed to be. Tom looked around, trying to see her, she knew, though he didn't know it was her he was looking for. Sheriff Dan followed the instructions to the letter. Leave the money on the side of the well facing the door. Then leave.

Carolyn watched until they were gone, then waited and waited some more. She had to be sure that they were really gone.

At dusk, she came out of the shack and picked up the money. She left the boy tied up. They would soon be on their way back to get the boy. She had to leave now. Had to be long gone by the time they got there.

She rode hard. The old hay burner that Sam gave her to ride didn't like to gallop and would only do it for a short while and then slow to a walk again. Carolyn dug in her spurs and got the horse moving. She kept at it to keep the nag going. She had to get out of there.

Carolyn heard the horses behind her before she saw them. She could barely recognize who it was. The sheriff, Dan Baker, along with Duncan McKenzie, the best tracker and an infamous bounty hunter. She cursed. She'd forgotten that McKenzie was friends with Tom. He was hunting her, not for a bounty but to help a friend. Either way she was screwed.

It was too dark to be running the horse but she had no choice. She whipped her mount with the reins and spurred it to go faster. Up, up the mountain, she had to go.

Suddenly, her mount slipped and went down on its knees. Carolyn screamed as she flew over its head.

Duncan came upon her first. With the lantern he carried, he saw her head was at an odd angle. Her neck broken.

"It's Sarah Harris. I thought she was dead. Didn't that low life she left here with send a telegram saying she was killed in a carriage accident?" said Duncan

"Yes, he did. So who was she in cahoots with? Who knew she wasn't really dead? And why did they wait all this time?"

"Ben isn't with her? Where did she leave him? Do you think she killed her own son?"

Duncan picked up her body, put it over the saddle of her horse and tied it down. The horse was badly winded and had skinned knees from where it hit the ground, but otherwise seemed alright.

"I don't know what to think. Let's go back to the shack where the money was left. We probably should have checked it first," said Dan.

"We found her tracks before we got to the shack. We didn't know that Ben wasn't with her. You follow me." said Duncan. "I'll lead her horse."

"Go slow. We don't want any more

accidents."

"No, we don't. We need to find that boy more than anything, but slow is better than never."

They walked their horses. Duncan in the lead, following the tracks back to the cabin. The trip was a lot longer than before because their pace, while leading the horse, was so slow. Dawn rose over the eastern ridge by the time they finally reached the old shack.

Inside, tied by his hands and feet with a gag in his mouth was Ben Harris. He looked up at Duncan and tears rolled out of his eyes. Duncan undid the gag and cut his hands and ankles loose. As soon as his ankles were free, Ben threw himself into Duncan's arms.

He held the boy until his sobbing stopped.

"Mama came to the ranch and got me. And...and..." he hiccupped. "I missed her so much, I went with her. As soon as she got me here, she tied me up," he sobbed. "When I started to cry she gagged me. Why? Why would my Mama do that to me?"

He held Ben away from him for a moment. "You're mama was a very bad woman, Ben. But you're okay now, and she'll never be able to hurt anyone again."

They walked outside. Duncan kept himself between Ben and the horse Sarah was tied to so Ben wouldn't see his mother. He saw her anyway, and Duncan watched Ben shudder before he buried his head in Duncan's side.

"You ride with me, buddy." Duncan lifted him into the saddle. "Dan, would you lead the other horse and stay behind me?" He nodded toward Ben.

"Sure thing."

They walked the horses until it was full daylight and then broke into a gallop. Ben needed to be home with his parents as quickly as possible.

*****

Tom paced back and forth across the room while she sat with Suzie asleep on her lap. Rosie refused to put her to sleep in her bed. Instead, held her in her arms, safe and sound. It wasn't logical, but it felt right. She wanted to hold her and squeeze her just to make sure she was safe.

What was Ben going through? What if the kidnapper hurt him? What if they hadn't had the money? All the bad things that could have happened went through Rosie's mind. What must Tom be going through? She looked up to where he stood by the window, staring out, just as he'd done every time he'd paced to the window and back to the fireplace. Back and forth, like it would bring Ben home quicker if he did.

This time when he paced to the window, his stance changed. He came to attention and pulled back the sheer curtain further.

"They're back. They have Ben!" he shouted, waking up Suzie.

Rosie soothed Suzie and got up, carrying her, walking as fast as she could while holding the child.

"Ben!" Tom yelled, as he ran down

the porch stairs.

"Papa!" Ben slipped down off Duncan's big black horse and ran to his father, leaping into his open arms.

For what seemed the longest time, they just held each other. Both crying. Father and son.

Silent tears rolled down Rosie's cheeks. Now that Suzie was awake, she wanted down. Rosie set her on the ground and she dashed to her father and brother. Tom bent down and picked up his daughter, then the three of them hugged each other.

Rosie understood. She really did. She was still the outsider. Maybe she would always be the outsider. After all, they shared a bond that Rosie couldn't, no matter how much she wanted to.

She turned to go in the house.

"Rosie." Tom's hoarse whisper reached her ears.

"Tom."

He held his arm out to her. "Come."

She bit back a sob and flew into his arms. They were a family.

A short while later, they were all inside, including Duncan and Dan. They listened to Ben, who sat on his father's lap, Tom's arms around Ben's body like he never intended to let him go again. She'd fixed Ben some food. He hadn't eaten since before his mother took him.

"It was Mama. She came and said I should go with her. That she'd missed me and came back for me." He looked up at his father. "I missed her so much, Papa. I thought we would be back for the rest of you later. I didn't know," he buried his face in his father's shirt.

"It's all right, Ben. You didn't do anything wrong. Mama's mind wasn't right. But she won't be hurting anyone, including herself, anymore. Do you understand, son? You're safe now. I have you and I'm never letting you go." Tom hugged the child in his arms. If it was Rosie, she'd be hugging him, too.

"Ben," said Rosie. "You need a bath, young man. It will make you feel better.

You can wash off all the grime from the last two days. Come with me and let the men talk. I'll help you get your bath started. Suzie, you come with me, too."

"I don't want a bath," said Ben.

"Go on, son. Rosie's right. You'll feel better. Then we'll get you some milk and cookies before bed. How's that sound?"

Ben smiled up at him. "Pretty good. But I don't need *her* help for a bath. I can do it myself."

Rosie wanted to insist, but instinct told her Ben needed this small thing to prove to himself he was okay. That and the fact that Tom shook his head when she'd looked up at him.

"Okay. How about I make some hot cocoa to go with those cookies?"

"I guess that would be okay," mumbled Ben, and then he marched up the stairs, with Suzie following, chattering at him like she always did.

Rosie looked at Tom. "What did I do?

He's so angry at me."

"I think right now he's thinking that his mother and I would be together if not for you, which in a way is true."

"What?" asked Rosie, crestfallen. After all they'd shared, he still wanted Sarah.

"It's not what you're thinking. I don't want Sarah." He came over to her and squatted in front of her. "I want you."

"Then what do you mean?"

He took her hand. "Things would have been different if I'd known Sarah was alive. I wouldn't have advertised for a wife, I wouldn't have met you much less married you…or anyone, because I would still have been married to her."

Dan spoke for the first time since Ben had started telling them his story. "We got the money back, but I don't think Sarah was in this by herself. She had to have someone in town help her, and I think I know who."

"Well? Who was it?" asked Rosie.

"Sam Kent."

"What? No way. Sam was nothing but helpful," protested Tom.

Dan leaned forward, rested his elbow on his knee and lowered his voice, assuring that his voice didn't carry beyond the room. "First, I recognize the horse she was riding as one of Sam's. We weren't supposed to ever see the horse, so I'm sure they thought it didn't matter. Second, it's too early for the mine payroll to come in. It's not due until next week. I keep track of when it's due in case something goes wrong. So Sam ordered cash in for another reason. I bet if we went to Sam's house, we'd find Sarah's city clothes."

"But why? Why would he help Sarah?"

"That I don't know. Maybe she was sleeping with him. Whatever the reason, we better figure it out before he finds out Sarah's dead."

Rosie listened to the men and then said, "Why did they target us? Sure, money was the main reason, but I think getting even was another. Sarah was supposed to be dead, but the idea that Tom remarried must have goaded her and then, when it turned out I was rich, well, Sam told her and one thing led to another. Which means he knew Sarah wasn't dead."

"Dan, you'll have to get into Sam's house. You have enough reasons to do it. Perhaps we need to go into the bank and redeposit the money so Sam knows the plan failed. I think he might try to run," said Duncan.

Dan rose from his seat at the kitchen table. "I'm going to have to take Sarah's body in, so she can be buried. If we don't catch Sam at something besides failing to report a stolen horse, he's going to get away with it."

"That can't happen. We have to do something. There has to be a way," said Tom.

"What if we left him a note under the door of his house, telling him to meet at the shack if he wants his share? That's all we'd have to say. If, as we suspect, he was a part of this, then he'll already know what shack to meet at," said Rosie.

"That's a good idea. We still have his horse. We can tie it up outside the shack so he'll think Sarah is still there," said Duncan.

"And when he goes inside to get his share of the ransom, you and I'll be there to greet him," said Tom.

"You don't think he'll wonder why or how Sarah could come all the way back to town to leave the note?" asked Rosie.

"I don't think he's that smart. Nothing about this seems very well planned. They saw an opportunity and took advantage of it. What I can't figure out is how Sam knew Sarah was alive," said Duncan.

"I want to ask Sam that question myself," said Tom.

Dan slapped Tom on the back. "We'll get answers. I promise."

Tom nodded.

"I'll write the note."

She wrote:

Change of plans. Meet me at the shack for your share. Tomorrow night at eight.

She let the men read it. "That should do it, don't you think?"

"I think so," they agreed.

"Now, who do we get to take it? If any of us show up in town and Sam sees us, he'll know his cover is blown and get wise that the ransom didn't work," said Dan. "He'll run and we'll never catch him."

"Who's the newest of your ranch hands?" asked Rosie.

"That would be Bart. He's only been with me for a few months."

"Then Bart it is. He's not likely to be recognized and associated with this ranch if he gets seen," said Rosie.

Tom took the note to the bunkhouse and gave it and the instructions to Bart. If he left in the morning, he'd get there while Sam was at work. Sam wouldn't find it until he gets home from work and would still have enough time to get to the shack before dark for the meeting.

Tom and Dan left after breakfast for the shack, just in case Sam got the note sooner than expected and decided to ride up there early. Tom rode Sam's horse. As planned, they tied Sam's horse out front. Dan tied his mount deep in the woods so there was no way to see it from the old cabin. And then they waited.

"Have you told her yet?" asked Dan.

"Told who what?"

"Don't be dense. Have you told Rosie?"

"What am I supposed to tell her?"

"That you love her."

"What makes you say that?"

"A man doesn't spend the money for the bridal suite at Mary's unless it's for the woman he loves. Besides that, I've seen the way you look at her and the way she looks at you."

Tom squirmed in his chair. "How does she look at me?"

"With her heart in her eyes. You know your marriage to Rosie isn't valid, right?"

"Not valid? I hadn't thought about it. We'll just get married again. Not a big deal."

"I think you'll find it's a very big deal to Rosie. She's seen the caring side of you. She's going to want, rightly so I might add, love on your part. She's earned it."

"Well I…"

"Rosie's a mighty fine looking woman. There are lots of men here, myself included, that would give anything to have Rosie for a wife."

Tom ran his hand through his hair. "What if I don't love her?"

"Then you should let her go. Let her find happiness with someone who does love her. She deserves that. She's worth it."

Tom shook his head. "I can't. I can't

let her go. The children love her."

"That's bullshit. They don't know if they love her or not. Right now, Ben only feels resentment toward Rosie. Regardless of how badly his mother treated him, he still loves her and thinks Rosie was in the way of Sarah coming home."

"Sarah's dead. For real this time. Ben knows that."

"It doesn't change his feelings."

"I'll convince Rosie to stay. Ben will come around."

"Yes, but will you? Rosie deserves a real marriage. You made it clear to everyone in town that you didn't want this marriage to be anything but a marriage of convenience."

"Things have changed."

"Then you better make sure she knows that, or you're going to lose her."

"I know…I... Did you hear that?"

Dan peeked through the hold in the wall. "It's Sam. Just as we thought. We'll grab him when he comes in."

Tom watched from his side of the door though a break in the mortar. Sam got off his horse and came toward the cabin.

"Carolyn? Sis?" he called out.

"Well, that explains it, doesn't it?" whispered Tom.

Dan nodded.

They stood on either side of the door. As soon as it opened, Dan grabbed Sam by the arm, twisted it behind him, spun him around and slammed him up against the wall.

"What's the meaning of this?" protested Sam.

"You're under arrest for kidnapping."

"Don't be ridiculous. I haven't kidnapped anyone."

"But your sister did, and you are an accessory to it. You helped her." said Tom. "I thought it was strange they'd ask for the exact amount Rosie deposited in your bank.

You're going to be spending a long time in jail."

"Total coincidence, I assure you."

"Right. And you showing up here after receiving a note from your sister is coincidence as well."

"Yes, I was out for a ride and…and…"

"Stop while you're ahead, Sam, and shut your mouth before I shut it for you," growled Tom.

"You can't prove anything. It's your word against mine."

"There are two of us and one is the sheriff, now you tell me who the judge and jury are going to believe."

Sam clamped his mouth shut.

The three of them went outside. Dan cuffed Sam's wrists together. They helped Sam onto Sarah's old nag and Tom got on the spirited stallion that Sam had ridden there. Dan handed the reins for Sam's horse to Tom and then went to fetch his own mount.

They walked the horses all the way back to the ranch in the dark.

Rosie was waiting up for them.

"I have a fresh pot of coffee or I can fix you some tea, if you prefer." She said to Dan as she eyed Sam. "I can see that we were right. But why? Why, Sam?"

"Sarah was his sister," said Tom. "We were married for almost nine years and I never knew she had a brother. She never mentioned having any family. I just assumed she was an orphan."

Rosie poured them all a cup of coffee, including Sam.

"What are you going to do with him tonight?" She nodded at Sam.

"I don't know. Maybe I'll cuff him to your cook stove. He couldn't go anywhere and he'd stay warm most of the night. And uncomfortable."

"I have a better idea," said Rosie. "Why don't you lock him in the pantry?

There's no windows or other doors, so he couldn't escape and you wouldn't have to stay up watching him. We'd put you in the guest room, Dan. It's just down the hall."

"Sounds good to me. I could use some sleep."

"Lord knows we all could. Here's the key to the pantry," she said, handing it to him.

CHAPTER 12

Rosie wore her silk negligee again and Tom made her take it off…again. She still thought it was the best investment she'd ever made.

Tom made slow love to her. He kissed her gently, reverently. Everything was slow. There was no hurry. He suckled her nipples and Rosie arched into his mouth. She pulled his head down, urging him to take more of her.

"Tom," she moaned.

She felt him smile as he pulled away with a resounding "pop". Refusing to release him, he acquiesced and laved her other nipple with attention. Lightly biting, then suckling, then starting over again.

He soothed his hand down her belly and opened her nether lips, plunging into her with one, then two, and finally three fingers. In and out he prepared her, loved her with his hand. She writhed under his ministrations, sighed her approval and silently begged for more.

His thumb rubbed her aching nub, bringing her all the wonderful shocks of awareness she so loved. She felt alive, really alive.

"Oh, God, that feels so good."

He moved down her body, scorching her skin with hot kisses. Before she knew it, his mouth was on her, licking up her slit, his tongue playing with her love bud, urging her to flower. To open for him.

"Yes. Yes. Yes." She exploded, bucking her body in rhythm with his clever tongue. Tom never stopped. He licked and sucked until she quieted. Replete. Spent.

Tom rubbed his rock-hard cock up

and down her wet slit.

"Wait," she said, stopping him before he entered her. "I have a question. Can I take you in my mouth and love you, like you do me?"

Tom got very still. "You would do that for me?"

She nodded. "I'd like to. I've been thinking about it for a while now, wondering if it is something you would like."

"Like? Like isn't the word I'd use. I'd love it. There's not a lot of women who want to love a man like that."

"Oh." She smiled. "Well, I'm not like a lot of women. I'm your wife."

"About that…"

Rosie put her fingers over his lips. "Shh."

Tom smiled and kissed her fingers. She replaced her fingers with her lips. "I love you." She whispered the words that had been in her heart it seemed forever. She wasn't sure he returned the feelings, yet, but at this moment it didn't matter. Right this minute all that mattered was she wanted to love him.

Rosie worked her way down his body with kisses and her tongue; she tormented him, just as he did her. She laved his nipples and then lightly bit them.

"Do you like that?"

He nodded. "Very much," his voice quiet and rough.

She continued downward in her quest, stopping to plunge her tongue in his belly button like he'd done to her.

Finally, she had his beautiful cock in her hand. She saw the bead of glistening liquid on the tip and licked it off.

"Rosie!" he groaned.

He sounded like he was in pain. She immediately stopped and released him. "Did I hurt you?"

"God, no. Please don't stop now."

Rosie smiled. "Good. Because I'm

just getting started."

She took the head of his penis in her mouth, pulled away and then took a little more. Each time she went farther down and took more of him. Then, she could take no more. He was hitting the back of her throat. She came all the way off him took him in again as far as possible.

She glanced up and found him watching her. His eyes, deep, dark pools of blue, urged her on.

"More. Suck me, baby, suck me."

Never one to resist a heartfelt request she did just that. Took him into her mouth and sucked and pulled back, not quite all the way off. Sucking as she went forward again until he pressed at the back of her throat and then out again.

"Play with my balls," his hoarse whisper urged her. "That's right, love."

She played and sucked and loved him with her mouth, learned the silky feel of his skin over the strength of his hard rod. Enjoyed him in a way she would never have thought possible before.

In too short a time, he gently pulled her up his body and then rolled with her onto her back.

"I need in you. Now!"

Delighted to have this effect on him, she spread her legs wide and welcomed him into her.

She was slick. Ready for him as he was for her. There was no gentleness. He slammed into her, burying himself to the hilt. His hot seed spurt into her and he ground out her name and then collapsed on top of her.

She welcomed his weight, clasped her arms around him and held him there. Time passed while their breathing returned to normal. It could have been minutes or hours, she didn't know. Finally, he lifted himself off of her and rolled to his side, taking her with him.

"Rosie, we have to talk."

"I know but I don't want this to end."

"We have to get married. Our marriage…"

"I know. It isn't valid."

"But if you knew, why did you make love with me?"

"Because I knew we'd be getting married again and…"

He smiled. "And?"

"And this time, I want a real wedding. I want to wear the wedding dress I brought with me. I want flowers. I want our friends there."

"Anything you want." He looked at her. "Why are you marrying me? I treated you like a slave."

"Yes, you did," she said as she played with the soft, curly hair on his chest.

"So aren't you afraid I'll do it again?"

"Nope."

"Why?"

"Because you love me now." She was so certain of it, she didn't even blink when she said it. It was true, she knew it in her heart.

"How can you be sure?"

"You got me Agatha, and you make love to me, not just have sex with me. Oh, yes, you're in love with me."

He chuckled. "You're right, I do love you. More than I ever thought possible."

"I knew it."

"And," he prompted.

"And what?" she feigned innocence.

He growled and squeezed her. "Rosie. And…"

"Oh, all right. I think I…like you, too."

He tickled her until she cried for him to stop. Laughing, she looked up at him and saw the vulnerability there. She stopped laughing and took his beloved face between her palms.

"How could I not love you? I think I have since the first time I saw you on the train platform. It was like I'd known you forever. As if I'd finally come home. Brusque as you were, I still knew. I love you, Tom Harris. Now and always. There is no other man in the world for me."

He relaxed at her words. "Ah, Rosie, I do love you. I have since I got your picture. I couldn't believe someone as beautiful as you would answer my advertisement. Then I decided to take a chance, to see if it really was you. I expected to see someone completely different on the platform and couldn't believe my luck, that it was really you. Then I realized I couldn't let you go, and decided to marry you immediately."

"You mean that wasn't planned?"

"Nope. The good reverend was as surprised as anyone when we showed up on his doorstep. But I had to keep you, and I thought marriage was the only way you would have stayed."

She cuddled sleepily into his side, "You don't have to worry anymore. I'm here forever. You and the kids are my life."

CHAPTER 13

The day of the wedding was well on its way. And coming too soon as far as Rosie was concerned. Catherine came and helped decorate the parlor with streamers and wild flowers in every kind of container you can imagine.

Rosie fried chicken until she swore if she saw another chicken she just might kill someone.

Tom slaughtered a steer and roasted it over an open pit in the yard for hours.

The whole valley was coming to celebrate and many to meet Rosie for the first time. Lots of townsfolk were coming, too. It was turning into the party of the year. Sadie closed the mercantile and Mary told her boarders they could come with her to the party or fend for themselves. Many of them were coming because they knew Tom and Rosie from their stays with Mary.

The only fly in the ointment was Ben. "Tom, you have to have a talk with him. He won't talk to me. He's still angry at me."

She was right. For the last two weeks, Ben was sullen and angry. If he spoke to Rosie, it was one word answers to her questions. Tom agreed it was time. He'd had enough, and this talk was long over due.

"Ben, you and I need to have words about your attitude, young man. You know your mama's leaving and her death were not Rosie's fault. Why are you so angry at her?"

"Because if she hadn't been here, maybe Mama would've stayed."

"No, Ben, she wouldn't have. Your mama left because she hated it here. She hated everything about her life here. She only came back to get money. Nothing else. You were a way for her to get that money."

"It was only because Rosie was here that she did what she did. She would have stayed for me."

"Son, she didn't stay the first time. Why would you think she'd stay this time?"

"Because she came back. For me."

"Listen to me, and listen to me good. Do you think your mama wanted anything except money? Would she have kidnapped you and tied you up? Would she have gagged you when you cried? Would she have done any of those things if she wanted to come back into our lives? There is no way to sugarcoat this, Ben. It's time you grow up and realize what kind of woman your mama really was. She wasn't a good person. She loved only herself. But, Ben, there is someone who loves you very much."

He looked up at his father, his eyes filled with unshed tears. "Rosie?"

"Rosie."

Ben let the tears fall. "Do you think she'll forgive me for the way I've treated her? I was just so angry, and I couldn't be angry at Mama. She was dead."

"I'm sure she will. She forgave me, and I treated her very badly when she first came. But she's still going to marry me. Marry us. Rosie is marrying all of us, Ben. You, me, and Suzie. We're a package."

"I love Rosie, too. I really do."

"Why don't you tell her that? I'll go get her and you can tell her here in private. What do you say?"

"Thank you, Papa. I'd like that."

"Be right back." Tom hugged his son.

A few minutes later, Rosie and Tom returned.

"Hello, Ben."

"Hello."

Suddenly he ran to Rosie and threw his arms around her waist, burying his face in her stomach. Crying, he said, "I'm so sorry for the way I acted. I'm so sorry."

"Oh, honey, don't cry. It's okay. I

understand."

"You forgive me?"

"Of course, I forgive you. I love you. You're my son now."

"I love you, too."

Tom watched as two of the people he loved most in the world cried in each other's arms. It was going to be all right.

"Rosie," said Ben between sniffles. "Do you think…I mean, would you mind…if I called you Mother?"

"Nothing would make me happier."

Tom stepped in. "Good. I'm glad that you two have made up. I have a question for you, Ben."

"What is it, Papa?"

"Would you be my best man when I marry your new mother?"

"Yes, sir." He sniffled and wiped his nose on his shirt sleeve. "I'd be honored."

"Good. Now we've got all of that settled, why don't you go see Agatha about some milk and cookies. Tell her you have my permission."

"Thank you, Papa." He gave Rosie one last hug before hurrying off down the hall toward the kitchen.

"Well, now, you're official. You're the mother of my children. Suzie already calls you Mama, and now Ben."

"He's had a lot to deal with. First me coming, then his mama coming back, kidnapping him, and then dying, practically in front of him. That's a lot for anyone to handle, much less a ten year-old boy."

"I know. I'm so proud of him."

"Me, too."

"So, soon to be Mrs. Harris, how about giving Mr. Harris a kiss?"

"Anytime, Mr. Harris."

Lowering his head, he took her lips with his. Then he caressed her breasts without breaking the kiss.

Rosie pulled back. "We can't. Not now." Then she gave him a quick kiss and turned to leave.

"I mean to finish this later, woman."

"I mean to let you." She grinned at him and sashayed out of the room.

*****

Rosie descended the stairs, and at the bottom of them took Ben's arm. Ben agreed to give Rosie away to his dad, and to be the best man, too. Rosie and Tom were both so proud of him. He'd grown up a lot in such a short time.

She wore her mother's wedding gown. It was long-sleeved pink satin, with small seed pearls at the cuffs and the off-shoulder neckline.

The pink color highlighted Rosie's pale alabaster skin. The combs she wore in her hair had seed pearls that matched her dress. She used them to bring the sides of her hair up, then left the rest cascading down her back in loose waves to her waist.

As she walked down the aisle on Ben's arm, she watched the emotions play across Tom's face. Love, pride, and even desire, there, for the entire world to see.

Suzie sat on Agatha's lap until she saw her brother with Rosie, then she scrambled off and ran to her papa. Agatha tried to stop her, but Tom shook his head and said, "Let her come."

Tom and Suzie waited for Rosie and Ben at the hearth. Reverend Black stood with them. Ben walked her slowly up the aisle just like they practiced. What they hadn't practiced was having Suzie throwing herself at Rosie's legs when she and Ben reached the fireplace.

Rosie took it calmly, simply handed her bouquet to Catherine and picked up her daughter. She held Suzie through the ceremony. When it came to the point where the reverend asked, "Do you take this man," Tom stopped him and whispered in his ear.

The reverend smiled and when he commenced he said "Do you Rosemary Louise Stanton, take this family, Thomas, Benjamin, and Susan Harris to be your family, from this day forward 'til death do you part?"

"I do."

"Then by the authority vested in me by the State of Colorado and Mineral County, I pronounce you a family."

Tom kissed Rosie, Ben hugged her, and Suzie watched it all with her thumb in her mouth. Rosie gently tugged Suzie's hand and gave her a kiss on the forehead. "No, no sweet."

"I told you. I'm not sweet. I'm Suzie."

Everyone burst into laughter.

EPILOGUE

Nine months later

Tom paced back and forth across the floor.

Duncan said, "You'd think this was your first child."

"Not mine. Rosie's. What if there are problems? What if…"

"You worry too much. Catherine is with her and so is Doc Johnson. She's going to be fine." He leaned back in the chair and put his feet up on the coffee table.

"I know. But Rosie is so delicate."

The coffee Duncan was drinking erupted from his mouth. "Delicate!? Are we talking about the same Rosie? The one you nearly worked to death? Who never complained? Who married you anyway?"

"Yes."

Duncan choked on his laughter. "You've got to be kidding me. Rosie could have a baby and go back to work without breaking a sweat."

Tom stopped pacing. "You don't understand. Rosie is…"

There was a cry from upstairs and Tom took off at a run, taking the stairs two at a time. He went into the bedroom and saw Rosie holding their baby.

"We have a boy."

He went to her and kissed her. "Thank you."

"For what?"

"For loving me enough to forgive me.

For giving me back my life, my family, my joy."

"You're welcome, my love. Now, what shall we name our son?"

"What was your father's name?"

"Raymond Noah."

"Then Raymond Noah Harris it is."

Tom sat on the bed with Rosie and Raymond. Ray started to cry and Rosie put him to her breast, teasing him with her nipple until he took it.

"He appears to be hungry for his mama."

She smiled up at him. "No more than his father."

He leaned down and kissed her again. "I love you, Rosie Harris."

"I love you, too."

THE END

ABOUT THE AUTHOR

Cynthia Woolf was born in Denver, Colorado and raised in the mountains west of Golden. She spent her early years running wild around the mountain side with her friends.

Their closest neighbor was one quarter of a mile away, so her little brother was her playmate and her best friend. That fierce friendship lasted until his death in 2006.
Cynthia was and is an avid reader. Her mother was a librarian and brought new books home each week. This is where young Cynthia first got the storytelling bug. She wrote her first story at the age of ten. A romance about a little boy she liked at the time.

She worked her way through college and went to work full time straight after graduation and there was little time to write. Then in 1990 she and two friends started a round robin writing a story about pirates. She found that she missed the writing and kept on with other stories. In 1992 she joined Colorado Romance Writers and Romance Writers of America. Unfortunately, the loss of her job demanded she not renew her memberships and her writing stagnated for many years.

In 2001, she saw an ad in the paper for a writers conference being put on by CRW and decided she'd attend. One of her favorite authors, Catherine Coulter, was the keynote speaker. Cynthia was lucky enough to have a seat at Ms. Coulter's table at the luncheon and after talking with her, decided she needed to get back to her writing. She rejoined both CRW and RWA that day and hasn't looked back.

Cynthia credits her wonderfully supportive husband Jim and the great friends she's made at CRW for saving her sanity and allowing her to explore her creativity.

TITLES AVAILABLE

TAME A WILD HEART
TAME A WILD WIND
TAME A WILD BRIDE
TAME A SUMMER HEART
CAPITAL BRIDE
HEIRESS BRIDE
FIERY BRIDE
LOVE AND MISERY, a very short story

WEBSITE – www.cynthiawoolf.com

SNEAK PEEK

TAME A WILD HEART

PROLOGUE

John Morgan's heartbeat drummed in his ears. Keeping a tight rein on himself so he wouldn't shout with elation, he looked down and watched the sunlight sparkle off the tiny yellow nuggets resting so unassumingly in his hand. Never had he seen anything quite so deadly wrapped in such a pretty package.

He'd been looking for it, for so long. Father never believed there was gold in this country, but he knew better. Too bad he couldn't have the satisfaction of saying 'I told you so' to the old man, but he was long gone now, not that it mattered. Only the gold mattered. The bright, glittering stones were the answer to everything.

Looking around again to be sure he was alone, he calmly carved his mark in a tree, so he'd know where to return. Yes, the gold was the answer to all his dreams; all he had to do was get the land where it rested. Not an easy task, for he knew he stood on the Evans' property. But the gold had always called to him and now that he knew where it was, he could answer. It didn't matter how; he would get this land and his gold.

CHAPTER 1

Flames licked through the canvas wagon cover. Great billows of black smoke escaped through the top. Horses whinnied. Men shouted. Cattle bawled. The scene was utter chaos.

Catherine Evans shouted orders, turning as a big black stallion charged into the fray. The large man on his back countermanded her orders and barked out his own.

Duncan McKenzie.

Nudging her own stallion, Wildfire, with her knees, she intercepted them. "This is my ranch and my men. I give the orders here. Where the hell have you been? You're a week late."

"I came when I could." Duncan turned to join the men.

"No, you stay." She whipped around to face the men beating at the fire on the wagon. "Forget the wagon. It's lost. Get those cows. Now."

After the men scattered she rounded on Duncan. "When you could, isn't a good enough answer. This is a working ranch. I have to be able to depend on every man here. And if I can't, then I don't want them. I don't even know why Dad sent for you anyway. We don't need a gunslinger."

"James has his reasons for asking me to come. As for needing a gunslinger, that has yet to be seen."

She disregarded his response. "You know about field dressings and I've got a man missing and probably hurt. Zeke was driving one of these supply wagons. I could use your help."

She galloped to the other side of the camp, riding around debris thrown from the supply wagon. Burlap sacks once full of coffee and beans littered the ground beside empty flour and sugar sacks. Tinned food lay bent, smashed under cattle and horse hooves.

Ignoring the destruction, she went straight to an overturned supply wagon.

Duncan reined in beside her. "The whole place looks like a battlefield."

"It is a battlefield and if you're here to help, then do it."

"I don't see anyone."

She stopped rifling through loose pieces of debris and cocked her head toward the wagon. "Did you hear that?"

There was a weak and distant groan. Catherine saw a muddied, work worn black boot sticking out from underneath.

"It must have upended during the stampede. Zeke was driving. We have to get him out." She let out a shrill whistle and Wildfire came running to her side. "Good boy."

She freed her lasso from the saddlehorn, dallying up the front wagon wheel. Duncan did the same to the rear wheel.

"Let's flip the wagon over. When I holler, you have that horse of yours pull."

She made sure both ropes were tight.

"Now! Pull. You too, Wildfire, come on boy." The wagon came slowly up and over onto its wheels, wood creaking as it bounced on its axles but it held together in one piece.

She ran around the wagon to the man on the ground, checked for bullet wounds and found none. The wound on his head bled profusely, as they are want to do, but didn't appear too deep. Running her hands over him, she found his right leg broken. "Zeke, are you all right? Zeke, can you hear me?"

She looked up at Duncan. "It's broken. It'll need to be set before we can move him. I can't do this on my own. I don't have the strength to set the leg properly. Will you help?"

"Sure. I need two straight pieces of wood and something to bind them." He took his knife and cut Zeke's pant leg open to see how badly the leg was injured. She could see the bone hadn't broken the skin and there was no bleeding, so it wasn't as bad as it could have been. He could stabilize it enough to get the man to a real doctor.

Catherine returned with a couple of loose boards she'd ripped from the wagon as Duncan started to cut off Zeke's boot. He hesitated when Zeke moaned, clearly in agony.

"Miss Catherine, is that you? What happened?" He was in obvious pain, but still lucid.

She smiled at him and gently brushed the hair back out of his eyes. "I was about to ask you the same thing. You've got a broken leg and I know it hurts, but before we set it tell me what you remember. All I heard was the cattle rushin'. By the time I got out of the timber, it was all over."

Zeke closed his eyes. "It happened so fast. Roy Walker and his men rode in. Next thing I hear gunshots. I tried to control the team but the wagon got pounded by the cows and tipped...I'm sorry, I don't know what happened after that." He closed his eyes then opened them wide. "The team! Where's Abel and Bessie?"

She shook her head, "Don't worry,

they're fine."

Zeke nodded then looked at Duncan. "Who's this? A new ranch hand? Replacing me already?" He tried to smile, but winced in pain instead.

She patted his hand. "Don't be silly Zeke, you know you're irreplaceable. Besides, I can't let your Sarah and little Jacob go, so I guess you have to stay too. This is Duncan McKenzie."

"Mr. McKenzie, any friend of James Evans' is a friend o' mine." Zeke lifted his hand. "But if you continue cuttin' on my boot, I'm goin' to kick you with my other leg. They're the only boots I got."

"Pleased to meet you. I've got to get this boot off so I can set your leg and if you kick me I'll have to knock you out."

"No way." Zeke ripped his hand from Duncan's and tried to rise, but Duncan held him down.

Catherine grabbed Zeke's hand and gently held it. "Don't worry. I'm gonna buy you the best boots in Creede. I'll make Gordon send all the way to Chicago if I have to. I'll even make sure that Jacob has a pair to match his Daddy's."

Zeke stopped struggling and relaxed. "The best, huh?"

"The best. I promise,"

"Catherine's promised and I'm a witness. Let's set your leg and get you home."

"Can you hold him down while I set it?"

She took a deep breath and nodded.

Duncan turned to Zeke and said calmly, "This is going to hurt like hell, but I've got to do it. I'll be as quick as I can. Yell, if you want."

"Here, bite down on this, it'll help." Catherine handed him the leather sheath from her knife.

"Just get it done." Zeke closed his eyes, put the leather between his teeth and locked his jaw.

"Wait a minute. You'll need something to bind it." She pulled her shirt from her pants and tore two strips from the bottom. She laid the cloth next to the boards within Duncan's reach.

"All right, hold him still." Duncan pulled hard with both hands to set the bones back into place, while Catherine put all her weight on Zeke's shoulders to hold him down. Placing one board on either side of the leg, he tied them tight with the strips of cloth from her shirt.

Zeke had not uttered a sound. He'd fainted.

SNEAK PEEK

TAME A WILD WIND

CHAPTER 1

Cassandra 'Cassie' Ann Drake
O'Malley pulled her little black buggy
through the gates of the Circle M ranch, past
the bunkhouse and the ice house into the
yard in front of the main house. Catherine
and Duncan McKenzie were expecting her
and waited on the wide porch that wound
around the entire house. Their son, Ian, age
ten waited by the hitching rail to tether her
horse.

"Ian!" RJ hollered. Cassie's son,
Raymond James, called RJ, jumped off
before the small conveyance came to a stop,
much to Cassie's exasperation.

Ian, who had the blue eyes and dark
hair of their father, grabbed the reins Cassie
tossed his way and wrapped them around the
hitching rail, then slapped his friend on the
back, much as their fathers used to do. "RJ,
good to see you. Come look at our new
colt."

The McKenzie girls Elizabeth
"Lizzie", aged seven and Mary, age three,

were not to be out done by their brother and ran down the porch steps, their red hair bouncing and shouted, "Sarah!" in unison.

"Sarah Jane O'Malley! You will not jump off this buggy." Cassie admonished and grabbed the little girl, who was a miniature image of Cassie, before she jumped and hurt herself.

Duncan rushed to help Cassie down but took Sarah Jane first. "Here you go, baby." he said as he set her on the ground and she took off running for her friends.

"Thank you Duncan. She forgets she's only two. She thinks she can do everything RJ does." said Cassie

Cassie put her hands on Duncan's shoulders and let him lift her down. Even though he was just a friend, it was nice to feel such strong muscles beneath her fingers and strong hands on her waist. Even for a second. Nice to remember she was still human. Not so nice to remember how lonely she was.

"Come on in Cassie before Catherine has a fit," said Duncan.

The lady in question ran down the steps as quickly as her bulk would take her. Catherine McKenzie was due to give birth to their fourth child at any time. Cassie loved her friend but was envious of her. Though Michael seemed happy with the one child they'd had she'd always wanted more children. She was pregnant with Sarah when he'd died almost three years ago and would love to hold a sweet babe in her arms again. If Michael hadn't died she might have had another baby. She guessed she'd have to settle for holding Catherine's right now.

"Cassie! I'm so glad you're here. I swear I'm going to have this child tonight, I hope you brought extra work clothes," said Catherine hurrying her friend up the steps and into the house.

Cassie had always liked the house that Cat and Duncan built. It was two story as most were in those days. All the bedrooms were up stairs. Downstairs they had done differently. There was what they called a great room. It was the kitchen, dining room and parlor all in one huge room. There was also another bedroom and an office down stairs. The great room was to the left of the stairs to the upper level. The office and fifth bedroom were to the right of the stairs.

"You know I always pack extra, when I come. The kids never stay clean and I want them in their play clothes until we all head to town." Cassie looked at her friend. "It looks like we may miss church this week. Are you all right? I think you should go put your feet up. Come with me."

Cassie put her arm around Catherine's waist and guided her to the sofa. "Now, you sit there and let me go make you some nice chamomile tea." Cassie turned to Duncan. "Sit here with your wife and don't let her get up. Why didn't you send someone for me sooner. The babe has dropped and I think we may have a little one soon, maybe tonight."

Duncan's face paled. He was always nervous when Catherine was about to give birth. You'd think that after three, the fourth would be no problem, but it was always the same. And at that point, he forgot he was responsible for putting the babe there in the first place.

"Duncan, pull yourself together and get that footstool over here for her feet.

Goodness Cat," Cassie admonished. "Haven't you been keeping your feet up like I told you to? Your ankles look swollen twice the size of normal."

Cassie rushed to the kitchen to start the kettle to boil. She had just starting to pump the water into the kettle when she heard a deep, baritone voice coming from the back door.

"Would you like some help with that?" he said.

Cassie dropped the kettle into the sink. "Don't sneak up on a person like that."

He didn't wear a hat and had obviously been washing up for dinner on the back porch. His damp brandy brown hair glistened in the kitchen light. When he got closer, she looked up, way up, into amazing emerald green eyes.

"Sam Colter, ma'am. Sorry to have startled you." He held his hand out to her.

"Cassie O'Malley." His large warm hand enveloped hers. She got a shock of awareness from his touch. Something she hadn't felt in years, passed between them. Something she hadn't felt since Michael had died.

"I've been hearing your praises, Mrs. O'Malley. Since I arrived yesterday, Catherine has been doing nothing but talking about you."

Cassie felt the heat creep up her neck. "I'm sorry I can't say the same, Mr. Colter."

"No problem. I wasn't expected, or I'm sure Cat would have been singing my praises to you." He leaned over conspiratorially and whispered. "I think Catherine fancies herself a matchmaker."

Cassie laughed. "That she does. You're not the first man she has thrown at me. Sorry about that."

He chuckled, a rich sound that traveled up her spine and settled in her chest. "I don't know if I should be flattered or insulted."

Made in United States
Troutdale, OR
09/07/2023

12707655R00156